AMERICAN PURGATORIO

Also by John Haskell

I Am Not Jackson Pollock

AMERICAN PURGATORIO

John Haskell

CANONGATE
Edinburgh · New York · Melbourne

First published in Great Britain in 2005 by
Canongate Books Ltd, 14 High Street,
Edinburgh EH1 1TE

First published in the USA by Farrar, Straus and Giroux in 2005

The author would like to express his gratitude to the MacDowell
Colony, where parts of this book were written.

British Library Cataloguing-in-Publication Data
A catalogue record for this book is available on
request from the British Library

Hardback ISBN 1 84195 597 3

10 9 8 7 5 4 3 2 1

Paperback ISBN 1 84195 639 2

10 9 8 7 6 5 4 3 2 1

Typeset in Times by Palimpsest Book Production Limited,
Polmont, Stirlingshire
Printed and bound in Great Britain by
Creative Print and Design, Ebbw Vale, Wales

www.canongate.net

For my parents

I

Superbia

1

I'm from Chicago originally. I went to New York, married a girl named Anne, and was in the middle of living happily ever after when something happened. I didn't know what it was, and if you would have asked me at the time I would have said nothing, that nothing was happening, because for me nothing was. I was standing in a convenience store next to a gas station along a picturesque parkway in New Jersey. I was perusing the assorted candies and snacks, debating with myself what to bring back to Anne. She was waiting in the car. We were driving to her mother's house and I was probably reading the labels, looking for something nutritious to eat. Although it wasn't a dream, the unnatural light of the convenience store made it seem as if I was existing in the *world* of a dream, the main difference being that, unlike a dreamworld, in this world, the convenience store world, nothing much was happening.

That's not right. It was all happening, I just wasn't seeing it. I wasn't seeing it because my attention was absorbed by walls of refrigerated cases and the aisles of bright displays. I was concentrating on all the possible choices, which, after a while, I'd narrowed down to a thin pack of peanuts, a protein-style candy bar, and a so-called energy drink. When I paid the cashier I didn't notice the rings on the woman's fingers, and I didn't count my change. When I walked to the door I didn't notice the grease stains on the square brown tiles or the sky which was blue through the window. When I walked outside, back to the car, all I noticed was that the car was gone.

This is a story of a man who . . . I won't say I was *never* stuck, but I was good at making adjustments. That was my specialty, adjusting to circumstances—I prided myself on this ability—and so the first thing I did was convince myself that nothing had happened, that Anne would suddenly appear. And when she didn't appear I began looking for her. She had to be somewhere, in some part of this service station area, and because there were only a limited number of places she could be, I kept looking in those places. I expected to see her, either waiting for gas or putting air in the tires or parked in the lot behind the small store. Although I didn't actually see her in any of the places she ought to be, I knew she was there in one of them, and that in my mind I was making a mistake, that fatigue or oversight or an optical illusion was keeping me from seeing what must be right in front of me.

According to our plan Anne would be filling the car with gas and I would be buying some treats for the road, for our journey to Nyack, north of New York City. New York City was where we lived, in a house in Brooklyn. We were driving to Anne's mother's house, and now she was parking the car, or had parked it, and was waiting for me in the parking area behind the store. But she wasn't there. The service station compound was not that big, and as I walked the length of it and took an inventory of every car, I could see that *our* car, our little maroon station wagon, wasn't getting gas and it wasn't getting air and it wasn't waiting in the parking area.

Something was happening. I wanted nothing to be happening. I wanted not to be nervous and worried, and although I *was* worried, I tried to keep that worry safely below consciousness.

4

Which wasn't easy. To keep it there I had to assume certain things. I had to assume that Anne was having trouble with the car, that she needed to keep the engine running, that she'd gone ahead and would soon be returning. Although this didn't make much sense, I was willing to believe it. I was eager, in fact, to believe it, because if it wasn't that, then it was some alternative, and I didn't want to think too hard about any alternative because I wanted her back. I wanted the car to be where it ought to be and I'd just overlooked it. There it is, I wanted to say. No problem, I wanted to say, but it wasn't the case. The car was gone and so was Anne.

I could tell I was upset because my heart was pounding against my chest; for me, that's always an indication. Also, there was the fact that I was cursing her, cursing, and at the same time praying for her safety. She wouldn't just leave me like that or forget me. That would be impossible. And yet if I let myself think about what might have happened . . . But I didn't do that. I should say, I didn't *want* to do that, because how could I not? How could I not imagine that some man with a gun or a knife had approached her and forced himself into the car, forced her to drive to some remote area off the road, some trees and a picnic table, and to lie on the picnic table, and she was wearing jeans, I could picture them, and her running shoes, and so the pounding of my heart was fear. I loved her and I was afraid. And yet at the same time if she was taking a little side trip to buy some . . . whatever, some film or some . . . sushi or something and she's, not raped, but safe and happy—although I wanted her to be safe and happy—I would be angry and was going to be angry, but at the moment I was confused, partly because I loved her and partly because I didn't want to feel the thing I was feeling.

Since I'd left my cell phone in the car I used a pay phone

by the air supply to call, first her cell phone and then mine, but either they weren't turned on or they weren't working. So I waited. I sat on the perimeter of the gas station, literally on the edge of a galvanized metal railing, watching the procession of cars pulling up to the attendants in blue uniforms. There was never really a lull in the stream of cars, but during a relative lull I walked to one of the attendants and asked the man if he'd seen a maroon-colored station wagon, or a dark red station wagon, but the man, naturally, couldn't remember any one specific car. And not only that, he didn't speak much English. But he wanted to be helpful, so he called over a colleague who, although he seemed more in charge, had even less facility with the English language, which was my language. And because I thought I knew a little Spanish I tried to speak, about *un carro con una señorita. Buscando por la señorita*, I said, and the second man, who according to his shirt was named Ramon, after consulting with the other attendants, and after some gesturing—all the time monitoring the gas pumps—made it clear that something bad had happened. Something *muy malo*. And although I didn't want to hear about anything *muy malo*, I said, *Qué pasa?* which means, roughly, "What is happening?", not because I couldn't feel what was happening to me, but because it was the only way I knew to ask what *had* happened, to my wife.

Something had happened, that much I could translate. I couldn't be sure what it was, or how it happened, or who it had happened to, only that it seemed to involve several people and a couple of cars. I believed the men were probably telling the truth, but it wasn't *my* truth, and certainly not a truth about Anne. They were describing some *other* situation. There were millions of women in the world, and as the attendants were indicating the height of this specific señorita, and saying that

6

moreno (which means brown) was the color of her hair, it was clear they were saying that this woman was gone. *Nada más.* Which means no more, but no more of what? I didn't know. I was saying to them, and to myself, *No problema, no problema,* but the men were shaking their heads as if there was a *problema,* a *gran problema,* and I was backing away, thanking them and nodding, trusting that the whole communication process was impeded by the excitement of the re-telling, or by the impatient honking of the cars waiting for gas, or by the language barrier; somehow in the gap between us the message had been scrambled, and I was getting the whole thing wrong.

All I could think to do was wait. Anne could be impulsive, and the waiting itself was an attempt to preserve the illusion that nothing substantial had happened. I sat on the metal guardrail, trying to find the padding in my buttocks, watching the cars, one after the other, car after car, and by now it was afternoon. It wasn't afternoon before, but now it was, which meant I'd been waiting a long time. And all during that whole time I was still expecting Anne to pull up any minute, waving and smiling and ready to go. I drank my drink, ate the peanuts and the candy bar, and tried to adjust. I tried to banish the unpleasant thoughts I was having. And I did, to some extent. I noticed the trees, for instance, and the slow sway of their branches. I tried to fill my mind with the small moments that together comprised what I thought of as beauty. The clouds in the darkening sky, and the cool breeze . . . And I was able in this way to find a modicum of that beauty. Some. A little modicum, if that's possible. But it wasn't enough to dull my agitation. And because I was still agitated, I decided to take action. Action begins with intention, intention leads to decision, and as the sun sank lower into the sky I decided it was getting late. I called Anne's mother (no answer) and I called

7

our house (again no answer). I called Anne's cell phone one more time and then decided to go home, saving my reaction to what was happening for later.

2

I walked back through trees and rocks, along a trail overlooking the Hudson River. I walked across the river, on the George Washington Bridge, and about halfway across I stood, with the wind and the sky and the sun going down, leaning against the railing of the bridge, looking down to the water and the patterns in the water. I was following with my eyes the current of the river when a man took a spot on the railing about an arm's length away from me. The span of the bridge was enormous and in that entire expanse the man chose to stand close enough so that if I wanted to, I could reach out and touch the man. Which seemed to signal a desire, on his part, to engage in some form of interaction. But when I looked at the man, in his windbreaker jacket, he kept looking away, as an animal might look away, out to the distant spires of the mettlesome city.

To normalize the situation, or to normalize my own discomfort, I began talking to the man, mentioning conversationally that I'd lost my car, telling him about the gas station and about Anne's disappearance. I didn't go into much detail but I had a desire to speak, so I did. "I can't find my wife," I said, but the man didn't look up. Or rather, he did look up, but his look didn't acknowledge me. I couldn't tell if that look was directed at me, or at something beyond me, something in the soft hills of New Jersey. And because I wanted to create some fellow feeling I turned and surveyed those same hills, and when I couldn't determine what part of the landscape he found so compelling, I turned back. The man was staring, not so much *at* me as through me, so that I had the sensation, not of being seen, but of being seen through. And it wasn't that I was afraid of the man; if you had asked me I would never have mentioned fear. But I *was* afraid. Of my own transparency. What was unbearable was to not exist, and although I knew I existed, I attempted to prove that existence, to get some acknowledgment from the man that his world and my world were at least a little synonymous. But before that could happen, the man, in his khaki slacks and yellow jacket, started walking, and he continued walking, past me and along the pedestrian walkway. I wanted to stop him and say something about our common experience—"Nice view" or "Some river"—and in this way manufacture a degree of fellow feeling. But instead I straightened up, stepped away from the railing, turned, and walked back to New York City.

I caught the subway to Brooklyn, walked down the tree-lined street to my house, and I could tell Anne wasn't home because no lights were lit. And that's all right, I thought, she's probably out shopping, at our local market, a co-op market, and I walked inside, turned on the lights, and waited for her to come home. I listened to a telephone message from Anne's mother asking us to call her back, but I didn't call back, partly because Anne was the only person I wanted to talk to, and partly because I heard in her mother's slightly distraught voice the desire to believe that everything was fine—thereby indicating that something wasn't fine—and the hope that if she believed it enough, everything would be.

Which was also what I was doing. I could accept the events that were happening as long as they meant what I wanted them to mean. While I waited for Anne to come walking in through the front door I tried to go about my normal life, to do what I normally would do, but I couldn't remember what that was.

I sat in my kitchen, our kitchen, with the little cactus plant by the sink. I sat in what I thought was my old familiar chair, trying to find its familiarity. I sat in a variety of ways—legs crossed, legs spread, legs up on the arm of the chair—trying to find the familiar position that would restore my familiar life, so that I could then live it. I was waiting for normalcy to return, and not just waiting, I was searching for that normalcy, and so I walked upstairs and went to sleep. I should say I went to *bed*, because sleep never came. I lay in bed, naked and slightly cold, the blue comforter pulled up to my neck, eyes wide open, staring at the uneven ceiling.

And Anne did not come home.

That night I woke, not from a dream, because I wasn't sleeping, but it was like a dream. In my mind I could clearly see a man—actually several people, men and women—getting into a car, my car, and driving away. I didn't know who they were, or remember who they were, but lying in bed, wide awake, I could see them. All night I watched a variety of permutations on the same basic story, a repetitious sampling of various people forcing themselves into the car, forcing Anne into the back seat or the front seat, and then the car driving off. To change these images, or control them, I tried to imagine a scene in which Anne uses some arcane martial art to subdue her assailants. When other thoughts intruded I pushed them away, fighting the un-welcome thoughts, trying to maintain the thoughts I wanted, the thoughts of Anne's superior power and cunning. These positive thoughts, however, were constantly shifting and moving, running ahead of me and getting away from me. I was chasing, in my mind, the images I *wanted* to see, and at the same time avoiding the unbidden images that were coming after me. And eventu-ally catching me. By morning I'd seen the scene, or thought it, so many times it became embedded into my reality.

In an effort to clear my mind I went to the upstairs front room, which was my room. I was going to sit on my antique rug and try to watch my thoughts for a while, or maybe watch my breath and forget about my thoughts. That's when the telephone rang. I walked down to the phone and listened for the message. It was Anne's mother asking Anne to call her back. Still trying to preserve the illusion of normalcy, I deleted the message, wrote it in the tablet we kept—a tablet made from leftover change-of-address postcards—and started boiling water for coffee. I made my coffee, buttered my toast, and sat at the kitchen table with my cup of coffee and plate of toast because that was my routine, and I wanted to preserve my routine— nothing like routine to dull the mind, although sometimes routine can sharpen the mind, like an execution or a knife.

What I mean is that my mind felt like a knife. The question—why I was sitting at this table without Anne—felt like the blade of a knife, and to avoid it I turned to my work. Before we'd left on our weekend getaway I'd spread out on the table a number of photographs, pictures of faces of babies. I was cutting out photographs for an article I was editing— for a baby magazine—about a baby's first year of life, and so I sat at the table, drinking coffee and eating toast, looking at the innocent cherubic faces and occasionally looking out the back window to the garden.

It was spring and the plants were starting to grow. One of the things—not the only thing, but one of the things—I enjoyed was looking out that old window. It was old and thin, and so the glass of the window had become like a sheet of water, like something fluid that almost seemed to be moving. And actually it *was* moving. The molecules of glass in a window do actually move over time, and instead of the seeming solidity of the glass, I was seeing the fluid. And through this fluid pane I was watching the green beginning of the season, the old maple tree in our yard and the ailanthus trees in the neighbor's yard, and I had in my hand a plate, a forsythia-patterned plate that she'd bought—that she wanted and we both bought—and I was brushing the crumbs into a pile on the plate, then pressing my finger into the renegade crumbs and eating them. In this way I was cleaning the plate.

And when the plate left my hands I didn't feel as if I was throwing it out the window. Not because it didn't feel like throwing, but because it didn't feel like *me*. Not who I thought I was, anyway. Some other me, I thought. And yet it *was* me. I did throw it. And the glass shattered, more than I would have expected, and the plate continued on its outbound trajectory, passing through the window and disappearing into the back-yard. I could feel the cold air being sucked into the warm house, or the warm air being sucked out into the cold, either way it had a cooling effect. The cold air that used to be outside was now surrounding me, and although it was getting cold, it wasn't *me* getting cold. I'd had enough of keeping the air out and the cold out and all the things I hated out, and now, like a huge inhalation, I'd taken the outside and brought it in, leaving me sitting there, looking through a broken window. I sat in my chair experiencing the transfer of air, feeling the temper-ature lowering against my skin, degree by degree, unable or unmotivated to do anything but notice it.

Or maybe I *didn't* notice it. Maybe I didn't feel the cold. Maybe a kind of pride allowed me to sit there and see what I wanted to see, see myself as what I wanted to be. Sitting at the table in the cold air, looking at the baby faces strewn across the table, maybe everything seemed fine or normal. The article I was working on was an attempt to make the difficulty of a baby's first year seem normal, to pacify and reassure and inform the readers (in that order) so as to create a world of acceptable reality and situate the reader safely in that world. A world I knew nothing about, by the way, a world of vomit and diapers that I had only *talked* about with Anne. And in the same way that I was manufacturing information about babies, I was manufacturing a belief for myself. Sitting at that round table I came to believe in what I thought of as a realization: the realization that Anne had been kidnapped. I imagined what had happened, and then talked myself into a belief in this version of events. Which relieved my agitation somewhat, and would have relieved it completely, except that now something had to be done.

I called the police but of course they told me there was nothing they could do. I said I wanted to report a missing person but they told me that their hands were tied, that I should sit tight and that my wife would eventually show up. I called Anne's mother again and again no answer, and although I didn't quite know what it was, I knew I had to do something. So I found some duct tape, gathered together most of the shattered pieces of window, and by taping the broken glass in the approximate location it had been before, I fixed the window, making it not good as new, but at least, as the day worked its way to its eventual end, there was action and movement, and although I was tired of being in my body, by fixing the window I was able to find a little normalcy. I wanted normalcy and so I interpreted the window breaking as a normal thing, saw the kidnapping of Anne as a normal thing, or at least a real thing. And I would deal with what had happened.

The odd thing was, as I sat in my chair looking at the duct tape repair job, I had no recollection of throwing the plate. As if some force had acted on me. In my memory the plate just seemed to fall, not down but out, at an angle, so that in falling, instead of hitting the floor, it flew like a thing with a mind of its own, into the window, as if trying to fly through the window, like a bird, blind to the pane of glass.

3

At this point the fellow who was never at a loss was at a loss.
I wanted to change something bad into something else, and I
attempted to do this by drinking bourbon from a bottle with a
faux wax seal, or possibly a real wax seal, it didn't matter because
either way, there I was, four o'clock in the afternoon, drinking
hard liquor as a way to stop what was happening. Although I
normally would have listened to the public radio station, I didn't.
I closed my windows, shut my shutters, and pulled a wool watch
cap over my ears to quell the sound of the cars outside, prefer-
ring instead to concentrate on what was happening inside, my
heartbeat for instance. I would have liked, if possible, to excise
myself from the outside world, or at least to push that world,
with its radios and telephones and honking cars, as far away as
possible, to do nothing but sit in the solid wooden chair (what
I called my lawyer's chair) looking out the broken window and
become like a plant in the garden, my hair growing and my
nails growing and that's about it.

Except that I had to do something.

I'd fixed the window. I'd stanched the flow of warm air out
of the house but I still hadn't stopped what was happening. I
still had to move forward, in some direction, and because I
didn't know what that direction might be, the only thing I could
think of was to take a nap. Not nap, but lie down on the bed.
Doing so, I thought about Anne and how we used to lie on that
same bed, warming each other, my legs over hers, or hers on

16

mine, and the sweetness of this memory was something I could only take so long—the fact that it was only memory, that all I had was memory, was painful—and then I got up, made coffee, sat in my lawyer's chair looking across the photos on the table to the empty chair in front of me. I imagined Anne, sitting as usual, her back straight, her feet wiggling, and it took some time before I realized that I couldn't keep talking, in my mind, to an empty chair.

So I walked upstairs and started looking around, first in the bedroom and then in her closet. She had a separate closet and her dresses and tops were all lined up. Stacks of shoe boxes were on the floor, and there were sweaters and scarves, and nothing seemed out of the ordinary. It's funny how we some-times act out the old banal clichés, because as I was standing there smelling the smells of the closet I leaned in and touched my lips to one of her dresses, a silk dress that I'd bought for her and given to her, and although she always said she liked it, she'd never worn it. In a box on the top shelf was her wedding dress, folded in tissue paper.

She had a small room in the middle of the top floor that she called her office. It had a skylight and a desk and I looked in the drawers of the desk. All her tax returns and receipts and operating manuals were filed in orderly manila folders. In the receipt file I found a yellow paid bill for a tune-up, from the Trinidadian mechanics we used. The date on the receipt was just six days earlier. She hadn't said anything about tuning the car, or that it needed tuning, but there was the receipt.

On the floor, in a stack of art books with the names of artists on the spines, one book didn't have a name. It was a sketch-book and only the first dozen pages were written in. More drawn in than written, mainly with geometrical shapes, cross-hatched ovals and polygons. There was writing on the top or bottom of the page, mainly reminders, things like *Call Dad*, or *Make stretchers*. She was an abstract painter, and other bits of writing were along the line of: *notice shades of green*, or *masks of faces on people like masks on baskets*, things that meant something only to her. Mainly there were just blank white pages, which in a way symbolized our life together. Just beginning.

There were a few papers on her desk, some unpaid bills, a folded map, and several postcard invitations to art-show openings. The map was a well-worn map of the United States and when I unfolded it there was a circle drawn with a felt tip marker around New York City. There was a line from New York to Lexington, Kentucky, which was also circled. As far as I knew she didn't know anyone in Kentucky. Or Colorado. The thick orange line followed the main highway to Colorado, where the town of Boulder was circled. The line stopped there, except that another circle, on the West Coast, was around San Diego, California. She was from San Diego. She was born there, which made the circle seem more than merely coincidental. It was her map, it had to be, and the cities she'd circled were . . . I didn't know what they were, and so I took the map to the kitchen. I spread it over the baby photographs on the table, trying to figure out what it meant, when the doorbell rang.

Patty, a neighbor who ran the community garden, was standing on the front stoop with her two black dogs, talking either to the dogs or to the woman standing slightly behind her. When I opened the door (and the dogs began sniffing) she asked if I wanted to participate in the neighborhood garden tour. They were looking for volunteer gardens to put on the list but I said I couldn't, that I was too busy. But Patty wanted to show her friend, a sturdy, older European woman, the backyard. "He has a beautiful camellia," she said, and without any invitation from me she stepped inside. She knew the way, and so she led her friend through the house, out the back door, and down the steps into my small plot of garden.

It was early spring, and as the two women named and commented on the various species of plants, the dogs played in the bulbs that were just coming up, trampling on and chewing slightly the hyacinths and daffodils and tulips. Thomas Jefferson said something to the effect that tending a garden makes a person grow younger, and maybe I was getting younger in some poetic way, but I wasn't *feeling* any younger, and in fact I was feeling tired. I watched the dogs and heard Patty calling the dogs, telling them to stop it and to sit, but I didn't really mind. I told her, *"No pro-blema."*

"What?"

"No problem," I said, and began asking the two women questions I'd had about tending a garden, and especially how to prune. I was in the mood for pruning, and it's possible that I heard what I wanted to hear because basically their lesson, as I heard it, was *prune with abandon.* They told me that plants enjoy being cut, that it's beneficial to their health, that it spurs their growth, and I probably wanted some control over something, and one way to have control is to cut things off. So that's what I did.

I waited until Patty had gone and then I kneeled alone in the dappled afternoon shade of the maple tree, examining the various botanical structures that were starting to appear in the garden around me. I looked at my rhododendron, standing against the fence, its buds preparing to flower. Despite the dogs, the daffodils and tulips were breaking through the porous earth. Green tips were sprouting on a pair of blueberry bushes. And because I loved the garden, and because the solace it brought was, in my mind, contrasted to the non-solace in my body, I held the pruning clippers in my hand, not like a surgeon, but I *felt* like a surgeon, examining a patient for signs of morbidity, looking to cure all forms of disease and death.

This is what I'm calling pride. I believed, along with a million other things, that I could control what the world was doing, and in my garden the world was beginning to grow. And it wasn't that I didn't want growth, I did, I wanted it, I wanted my garden to live and prosper, and that's why I held the clippers. To save something. To be rid of pain and fear, which was *my* pain and *my* fear, and although I anthropomorphized the dumb green garden, it was my own dull gnawing that was gnawing me. That was what I wanted to cut. But since I couldn't cut that, I turned to my plants, first the obviously dead branches, the ones that snapped because the life was gone, and then the partially dead, and then the ones that were alive now but that, at some point later, would be dead. And since everything, at some point later, would be dead, I had my work cut out.

And I'm calling it pride because I believed not only that the eradication of the bad could happen but that I could *make* it happen. That I could fit the world into my particular need, which, at the moment, was a need to cleanse some thing in me, some emotion in me, and yes, I was willing to adjust to the world, but I also wanted the world to adjust to *me*. I wanted the reality of that moment to leave my body, to float away like a breeze-blown vapor.

That's when I started cutting. And in this effort to soothe myself and rid myself of what I thought I needed to be rid of, I got carried away. The garden was my world, and to save it I began cutting, and the cutting led to more cutting, and I got lost in the cutting, bud after bud, leaf and twig and blossom falling— not like seeds, because they were dead now—but falling on the ground as I moved from rose to hydrangea to lilac, mindlessly and frantically cutting, so completely involved in the act of cutting, so absorbed in the belief in the beneficence of cutting, that I pruned to death every plant I ever cared about.

I was oddly methodical as I strode from plant to plant, from peony to camellia to forsythia, so numbed by the frenzy that was whirling around inside of me that I didn't notice what I was doing. Until afterward. That's when I saw that my carefully nurtured garden had been reduced in a matter of minutes to unliving stalks. That's when, exhausted and sweating, I sat on a step leading down from the deck and rolled for myself a thin tobacco cigarette. Because I wasn't a smoker, after about the second puff I got light-headed, and was just rubbing the butt in the dirt when the telephone rang. I'd been letting the phone ring since Anne had gone, but this time—something about the combination of dizziness and exhaustion and surprise—I forgot to let it keep ringing. I ran into the house to answer, and the next thing I knew I was holding the phone. Mike See, an old hockey buddy who'd apparently called before, was calling now, telling me about this car that was for sale.

4

I didn't need a car. I already had a car, and I told Mike I had a car, a maroon car, but he kept going on about what a deal this car was and how cheap it was, and as he kept talking I began to realize that in fact, at the moment, I *didn't* have a car. I didn't think I wanted a car but I asked him, as a courtesy, what the price was. He evaded the question of money, and emphasized instead the motivation of the seller, that the car just needed a little attention, and that he and I hadn't seen each other in a million years. In the course of the conversation I went from uninterested in owning another car to curious about this particular car, and when he said he'd get me a good deal, for friendship's sake, I told him I might be interested. And so we agreed to meet.

The next day I rode my bicycle to the Red Hook section of Brooklyn, down near the water, to an address I'd written on a piece of envelope. It was a moderately well maintained brick row house and in front of the house a faded red sports car, or quasi-sports car, a Honda or Nissan, was parked on the street. Mike appeared from under the stoop looking as he had years ago—a little heavier and a little slower—jangling the keys. "Let's go for a cruise," he said, throwing me the keys. I got in, adjusted the seat and the mirror, and began driving around the warehouse streets, and all the time I was driving Mike was talking, not about the car, but about the girl who was selling the car. She was a nurse, he said, and very friendly. "I've told her all about you," he said. "She wants to meet you," he said. And I assumed she wanted to meet because she wanted to sell her car, but the way he said it, or the way he *kept* saying it, made me wonder. We drove around in the cold sunlight and it was pleasant to be driving, and the car itself seemed a fine enough car, nothing exceptional, until Mike mentioned the owner's breast augmentation.

The expression "breast augmentation" sounded artificial coming from Mike, but even with its note of false sophistication the idea piqued my interest. I'd never knowingly met a person who'd changed herself in such an obvious and prominent way, and who, because of that change, was probably feeling optimistic about the future. I thought at the very least I should talk with her, about the car, and I wanted to talk with her. But when we got back from our drive she wasn't home, and so it was in my imagination that I envisioned her in her nurse's uniform. But because I had never seen this girl, the images in my mind were images of Anne. The breasts I imagined, naturally enough, were Anne's breasts. And as I rode my bike up Union Street, thinking about Anne and the car, if it hadn't already, the idea of Anne and the idea of the car became conflated. A desire was created for the thing that was Anne-and-the-car. And not only was the idea of Anne conjoined to the idea of car, but they both were connected in my mind to the general idea of breast augmentation. Although I was only dimly aware of the intricate psychological machinations it took to make that connection, it didn't matter. She'd left me the map because she wanted me to find her. She wasn't kidnapped. She was safe and alive, and there'd been some miscommunication or misunderstanding, something we could talk about. I needed to talk with her. If I could just talk with her, I thought, then maybe this whole thing didn't need to be happening.

From that point on I was a man on a mission, and like a man

on a mission I put my life in order. I shaved and showered and brushed my teeth. Like a man on a possible suicide mission I went to the bank and took out all my money. Whatever the car cost—Mike guessed about seven hundred dollars—I was prepared to pay, in cash, and the next day I took a bus to her house. When I arrived, Mike, waiting on her front step, informed me that his friend was in the shower, that she had to work at the hospital, and that I should give the money to him. "She wants me to be her agent," he said. And as I signed the various transfers of title, I tried to postpone the moment of payment as long as possible, talking with Mike about his thirty-two-year-old 1970 Cadillac Coupe de Ville, waiting for her to emerge from the house, not bikini-clad, but somehow revealing her transformation. But she didn't emerge. And yes, I was slightly disappointed, but only slightly. I realized that it didn't matter anymore about the person who *had* owned the car. It was my car now, and with it I had the ability to move forward.

I paid Mike and agreed to let him get the car, a Nissan Pulsar, "ready for the road." I would soon be taking a trip in which I would find Anne and bring her back, and for all I knew, it would be a long trip and I wanted the car in good condition. As I followed Mike to his garage I imagined Anne sitting in the front seat next to me. Like an amputee with a lost limb, I felt her and wanted her reconnected. And because desire breeds hope, I was optimistic. Anne was my object and my direction (my future) and I would use the car to find her. She was the woman who'd been separated from me, the woman I loved. And I say thank god for pride because pride was the soil out of which my belief was growing. Not only did I *want* to find her, but I *would* find her. Somewhere along the way the seed had been planted that this was the car in which what I wanted to happen (my belief) would become reality.

5

I'm thinking of a specific moment, six months earlier. It's a cloudless September morning. Light comes from the upstairs windows and we're lying in bed, still partly asleep. We open our eyes, reach out, and we find each other, warm and naked. We stretch our legs, untangling ourselves from the sheets, and in this way the day begins. You (the responsible one) get up first. You throw off the comforter and as you crawl over me I try to spank you. I hear you peeing in the bathroom. You wrap yourself in a robe and announce that we're going to have breakfast in bed. I can hear your steps on the stairs and I can smell the coffee brewing and the toast toasting and I arrange the pillows. I transform them into backrests so that when you bring up the wooden tray with the cups of coffee and plates of buttered and honeyed toast there's a space for you under the covers. And there we sit, looking out at the trees and beyond them to other trees, and talking. In the distance, dark smoke rises into the sky, but because we're talking—I forget what about—nothing matters except the two of us. We're talking about nothing and everything, letting our words, warmed by the coffee, come up from inside us. After the coffee comes the kissing. I kiss you and you kiss me, and in our kissing we release the memories of all our accumulated kisses. And like happy rats in a maze the kissing brings up more than memories. I glide down along your body, warm and forgiving, full of sensation and blood, and I do what I do and you do things, and our embrace just happens. Seemingly.

We *do* nothing, wrapping ourselves around each other and through each other, both inside and outside, following and leading, bringing each other to the metaphorical precipice of pleasure, balancing on that delicate ledge as long as possible, moving back and forth from the edge of that ledge, then falling off. And after another sip of coffee we silently pull the comforter back up over our bodies. Usually you put your head into the crook of my arm, but today is different. Today I curl up and rest my head on your slightly damp stomach. Actually a little lower than your stomach. I want you to breathe easily so I place my head partially on your belly and partially on your pubic bone. I close my eyes and I can feel your breath, rising and falling under me. Maybe we fall asleep, I don't remember, but we lie like this until, after a while, I feel you sliding out from under my head. You get up, get dressed, and start your day. But I don't move. I don't want to. I'm still feeling your belly, rising and falling. Although I've put my head on a pillow, what I'm feeling is you, your breath under my head. This is the moment I'm talking about, the moment I'm remembering. Although you're gone I'm still feeling you. And because I want to keep feeling you, I think that I will, forever.

6

When I say that desire breeds hope, what I mean is that desire contains within itself the seed of its possible attainment. As I sat on a wooden bench, waiting for Mike to finish fixing the car, I had the hope, but the problem with hope is its fragility, and because of this fragility, after a while my hope began to mutate into something else, something more substantial and secure. Where hope had been, now belief existed. The achievement of my desire became, not only possible, but certain. I believed my connection with Anne had been real and would continue to be real, and while this was a kind of pride, it wasn't necessarily bad. Without it, and without its attendant optimism, why would I think a high-mileage used car was anything other than a mass of sheet metal and rubber. I wanted to transcend its prosaic nature, and so I transformed the car from something prosaic into something transcendent, into a car that would find my wife. She would be like a beacon, and I would use the car to follow that beacon. And to mark my ownership of the car I took from my wallet a photograph of Anne, a shot of her in perfect focus, during a snowstorm, turning to the camera, the world behind her completely blurred. I borrowed some electrician's tape and taped the photo to the middle of the dashboard. At first it fell off, but I added more tape and eventually got it to stick on a suitable surface just above the radio.

Since Mike's job was to fix cars, he found a number of things that needed to be fixed. "I can fix anything," he said, and he raised the car up on blocks in his small garage near the Gowanus Canal. He took off the wheels to show me, with a screwdriver, the brakes or the shoes of the brakes, which he said needed replacing. He snapped the belts, which looked perfectly fine to me, but he replaced them. He replaced the oil and the hoses— "You don't want leakage," he said—and because he was an old friend, he threw in some fresh brake fluid. And because the idea of replacing the old with the new was philosophically appealing, I approved the repairs. I paid Mike when he finished, and as I was just about to begin my journey, just about to drive away, as I opened the door and was about to wave to Mike and settle into the low vinyl seat, he mentioned something about a poker game.

Well, I wasn't interested in games, and I said I wasn't interested. "I think I'll pass," I said, and although I said it, I didn't drive away. I got out of the car and waited until the players showed up, all of whom I knew. We shook hands, performed the requisite slaps on the back, and I explained to them that I was getting up early tomorrow and that I had to call it a night. But I didn't call it a night. I had the belief that I would find Anne, but I was beginning to think it might be a good idea to test that belief, to get a little confirmation.

The next thing I knew I was sitting at a round table covered in green felt, with Welters and Perper, Polizze and Mike, and Mike's brother, known as Bones—all friends from Stuyvesant High School. Although I didn't attend this particular high school I was part of their circle. And when the game began, for the first few hands, I got nothing. A few pairs, a few aces, but basically nothing. I folded quickly to keep my losses at a minimum. This went on for a while with some players winning, some losing, and all the cards seeming random and unrelated. Yet even when the hoped-for cards refused to materialize, my belief that they *would* materialize didn't abandon me. Instead it hardened into

28

surety, or a faith, in which I lost sight of the fact that I was losing, a fact I didn't want to believe. I was a winner, I thought. Born to win. And so I kept betting and kept losing, and anything is possible, I thought, and when the next hand of cards was dealt I ended up with three queens. I was sitting there, trying to look nonchalant, and I didn't bet much, or press too hard, but I won the hand and with it the money. And I began to feel good, to feel that some luck was coming my way. I knew enough to know that luck, or intuition, or harmony, moves in waves, and I could feel that a wave was gathering for me. And I won again. I won the next hand, and the hand after that, and now it was easy. And this is how, fueled by the facts in front of me (the cards on the table), my confidence was reinforced by reality.

And when the game ended, or when it ended for me, I left my winnings on the table. When I stood up and walked to the door I was feeling in sync, not only with the cards, but with the world. I knew it didn't always happen like this, but if a person pays attention, sometimes the underlying logic of the world is revealed, sometimes there's a convergence of desire and actuality, and because it comes in waves, it's possible to ride those waves. I said goodbye to my friends and walked outside. I walked from the round table into the cool, damp air, and standing there, I felt that convergence. The thing I'd been wanting to happen was finally happening. And sure, I recognized that it might not always be happening, but eventually it *would*. When it mattered, it would happen, and when it did, I would be paying attention. It didn't matter about winning some stupid card game. Winning a game didn't matter. What mattered was finding Anne.

7

I didn't want to think about probability. The probability, if I thought about it, of finding Anne before she got to Lexington was not that great. And yet I believed it could be done, knew, in fact, that it could and would be done. The worn-out map was an outline, and I would follow that outline to get close to her, and once I was close, then the world would tell me what to do. I would follow the dictates of the world, first by paying attention to the signs, and then by following them. Which signs? I would know them. How to interpret them? I would learn. The world was interconnected, so that in following the signs, and living under the sway of these signs, I would be following Anne's trail. To understand the world, I had to be part of the world, and I was determined to go into the world and, like Bach or Mozart or Charlie Parker, let the world play through me. I would read the world and communicate with the world and be directed by the world. And let the world tell me what to do.

That night, instead of sleeping, I loaded the car with the objects of my life. You wouldn't call it packing because it was a little too random for that. My goal was to travel light, and mainly I brought along things that reminded me of Anne. Most of it I knew I didn't need, but I packed these things, which included a cardboard box of paperback books, photos in an envelope, a sleeping bag, a laptop computer, a potted cactus, binoculars, clothes, cassettes for the car, and my father's mandolin. I packed all these things, along with my notebook, into the trunk and the back seat of the small car, and I knew I was probably leaving behind something important, but nothing that I really needed. It was late and raining when I locked both locks of the blue front door, got in the car, and drove away.

Before I drove away I sat in the car looking up through the rain-spotted window to my house, lit by the streetlight. I said goodbye to the place I'd painted and plastered and lived in. Then I turned, away from the house to the street, and beyond that to the city, and beyond that to something else.

I knew what I was doing.

My life was dependent on how well I paid attention, and so, as I drove through the nighttime city, I didn't mind the stoplights or the honking or the rutted road, because they were a part of the world. I was driving along on the elevated expressway, with the buildings of the city below me, listening to a Spanish-language cassette tape that either Mike or the nurse had left, a tape which, when it worked, acted as a white-noise background for thinking. *El gusto es mio, el gusto es mio.* I was thinking about Anne, and also thinking that a journey of a thousand miles begins at this exact moment, and the next thing I thought was that something was wrong.

As I said, it was raining, and as I was changing lanes I noticed that something was wrong with the steering. There was a lag time. I would turn the wheel, and then later, not too much but a little bit later, the car itself would turn. This led to overcompensating, which led to swerving, and because this was a problem I pulled off the highway, drove down the off-ramp onto a boulevard and into a gas station, where I parked under the bright fluorescent lights. I opened the hood, checked the few things I knew to check, and found that I was low on power-steering fluid.

When I walked into the office of the gas station—it was an old-style gas station with fan belts and air filters hanging on the wall—the first thing I saw were two chairs stacked in the middle of the room with a red coffee can sitting on the seat of one chair catching drops of water falling from a leak in the ceiling. There was a young man, a kid really, behind the counter and I said to the kid, "Excuse me, do you have any power-steering fluid?" But the kid didn't hear me. Or if he did, he didn't respond. He was wearing a pair of headphones. "Power-steering fluid," I said, waving my hands so the kid would notice me, but I seemed to be in a different world. The kid could see me and hear me, but I seemed to exist as if in a television set. I kept saying, "I need some power-steering fluid," telling the kid and waving at him, but the kid didn't respond. Then, at a certain point, he took off the headphones, came around from behind the counter, took the coffee can which was just about full, and put in its place an empty Styrofoam cup. And then he went through a door into some sort of back-room area.

Well, the first drop of water that hit the Styrofoam cup knocked it off the chair, and of course the water began dripping onto the chair and ultimately onto the floor, and I could see what was happening. The drops were beginning to form a pool beneath the chair. So I reached down, picked up the white cup, and held it, catching the drops of water as they fell. I was standing there, holding this cup, waiting for the kid to come back, and I saw the headphones sitting on the counter. I reached over, picked them up one-handed, and slipped them over my ears.

There was an interview going on with Itzhak Perlman, a noted violinist, punctuated with examples of him playing the violin. He was saying that he'd been playing since he was a baby and that the music was a vehicle for him, and I thought, This man is lucky. He didn't have to ask, What am I going to do? or, How should I do it? And even if he did, he had his music, which was his key, opening the door, not just to the world we know, but to parts of that world which are unknown. Once Itzhak Perlman became one with the music, once he and the world became the same thing, he could then change the world. And the only thing is, once he became the world, there was nothing to change.

And then the kid came back. He put the empty coffee can on the chair and took the cup from my hand. I put the headphones back on the counter, and the kid went around to the other side, put the headphones onto his ears, pulled out a bottle of power-steering fluid, and set it on the worn linoleum. "That's great," I said. "How did you know?" but the kid didn't respond. "How did you know?" I was asking, but the kid was just looking back, his eyes open but that's about it.

So I took the bottle out to the car.

Somehow the kid had understood what needed to happen, and it happened. And I thought that partially I'd made it happen. Somehow by my actions, by the *way* I held the Styrofoam cup, or the *fact* that I held the Styrofoam cup, I'd changed the world. I was feeling slightly euphoric, and this euphoria gave me a feeling of confidence or control—even superiority—over events in the world. It's possible that I was interpreting the world to suit my needs, and if I was, I didn't care. The world doesn't care *how* we see what happens, or *if* we see what happens. But it's all happening, and I was happening just as much.

I was standing at the gas pump, happy to be pumping gas, and it was all very normal, very mundane, and as I stood there, next to this fading red coupe, one hand on the gas nozzle, one hand on my hip, I looked around.

I remembered Anne.

I remembered that she was driving when we pulled off the

highway. Gas is cheaper in New Jersey, so we'd made it a custom to stop at that particular gas station on the Palisades Parkway. Although the memory was more like a dream, I remembered pulling into the line for gas, volunteering to get us something to eat while she waited in the car. When we drove we always liked to have a bite to eat, so I opened the door, I remembered that, put my feet on the hard cement, and as I'm getting out, another car, a gray car or silver car, moving rapidly, drives up alongside, about an arm's length from my open door, and only at the last moment does it veer away. I turn and I see the car (a luxury car) cutting to an open gas pump in the front of the line. As I walk past the car to the store I look in and I see a man driving and a woman in the front seat. I walk to the convenience store, buy the protein bar and the peanuts and the drink, so I have my hands full when I walk out, and she's gone. Anne and the car. Both gone. And the first thing I think, not think, but the first thing I do is curse. First curse, then pray. I hate waiting, and as I wait I'm thinking of what I'm going to say to her. Something about how could she leave me in a stinking, noxious, unbearable gas station. Not that I hated the gas station. I hated being left alone.

I poured in the power-steering fluid and finished pumping gas. From the vantage of the pump I could see, in the distance, the clouds, illuminated by the lights of the city, and the rain that was still falling. If I relaxed my concentration I could see the individual drops reflecting the light as they fell, and although the world had gone quiet, it was quiet in a way that was not completely peaceful. I should say that what was not completely peaceful was inside me. What was inside me was the fear of invisibility. I was trying to keep that fear, and the turbulence of my reaction to it, at bay. I knew, whatever it was, I could battle and beat it, and so I closed my mind. I wanted to preserve an illusion of who I was and so, although I didn't completely fill the tank, I started driving, out of New York City, and hopefully out of the past.

II

Ira

1

I thought I was going to drive all night, but instead I drove to that particular gas station in New Jersey. I pulled into the parking area behind the convenience store, adjusted my seat into the maximum recline position, and then I fell asleep. Or tried to. But it's almost impossible to sleep while at the same time *trying* to sleep, so instead of sleeping I just lay there, listening to the passing cars and reliving, and hating, and at the same time not quite knowing, what was happening to me.

When the morning light finally began to light the sky, the first thing I did, after a quick stop at the men's room, was walk to where I'd been standing when everything changed, the spot where Anne had disappeared. Standing on that area of asphalt, I let my senses take in as much as they could, hoping my intuition would find, in one of the myriad sense perceptions I was taking in, a clue to where she was.

The trees surrounding the parkway were beginning to display the first green shades of spring. Men were busy pumping gas beneath the shiny metal structure of the gas station. People were walking together holding hands. A thousand different events were circling around me, but like any of us, I could only make sense of a limited number of them. And none of them was telling me what I wanted to know. Which is why I got down on my hands and knees and began sniffing the asphalt. To utilize the underutilized sense of smell. And it wasn't the asphalt or the oil, or the gas or the doughnuts or anything present; it was a whiff of something that *had* been present, and now wasn't. By the time I stood up I knew what I was doing. I bought a medium coffee and a chocolate doughnut and I got on the road.

Driving along in that little red car, I probably looked like a typical human being, driving along, thinking about either the past or the future, or both. And I was. I was thinking about Anne (in the past) and our eventual reunion (in the future). I had the sense that Anne was out there pulling me. Like a bloodhound with the scent of some discarded scrap of clothing, I kept my concentration on the road, connecting myself to the road as if by a mental thread, and I was following that thread forward, which in this case was westward. "Westward-ho," I said under my breath, and then again, out loud, "Westward-ho!" I drove along the smooth wide highway, not stopping to eat because I had to make up valuable time, watching the road because that was my guide, but also watching the sky, and with my window down I was smelling the air. And it wasn't the smell exactly, because inside the car there was only the plastic smell of the cracking dashboard, but somewhere near an exit for Harrisburg, Pennsylvania, I got the scent of Anne, or the figurative scent of Anne, and I pulled off the interstate into the next rest stop. It was less a distinct odor and more a remembered redolence, like an image from memory, bright and brief and then fading. It was subtle, and I would have preferred something less subtle, something more substantial and palpable, but there I was, a man in a certain situation.

I spread Anne's map across the steering wheel, hoping to find on the folded piece of paper something that would synchronize the world on the map with the world outside the windshield. Although the yellow line on the map had a wide generalized swath, it was pretty clearly following the major highways. But what if she decided (or someone decided for her) to take a different road? There were hundreds of thousands of miles of road and Anne might be on any one of them. To follow the right path, you have to know what the right path is, and to know what the right path is there can't be a lot of distractions, and by that I mean emotional distractions that make the right path and some alternative path indistinguishable. There's always some path, and I was on my path, but I had the growing suspicion that I'd veered off the right path onto another path, a path that was parallel to Anne but didn't intersect with her.

I might easily have called it an impossible situation, but I refused to do that. I wouldn't let that thought, or anything resembling that thought, get even *close* to consciousness. I had to be clear, had to keep my mind like a radar. I had to believe, and I did. That I would find her.

I got back on the highway and drove. And as I drove, and as the hours went by, even the bugs crashing against the windshield seemed to confirm my fear that the world was conspiring, not *against* me exactly, but it wasn't *with* me, or I wasn't with it, and whatever conspiracy existed, I seemed unable to join. All I could do was follow my instincts, such as they were, hoping for a flash of inspiration. And after a while, in lieu of that flash, or anything resembling that flash, in an effort to do something other than not doing anything, I randomly chose an exit. I drove down a winding road which turned into a winding street that eventually led into a town.

Morgantown, West Virginia, was a once-thriving industrial town on a river, and it was still on the river, and now it had a university. I parked by a parking meter on a fairly lively street not far from the university and I put my head out the window. I was hoping to get some clue from the air, or some particles blowing in the air, but it's hard to smell any specific odor, let alone find meaning in that odor, when your mind is filled with the realization that you have basically no idea what you're doing. Which is how despair originates (from the Latin, *desperare*, meaning without hope) and what I did to forestall that despair was to imagine Anne.

The only problem was, every thought I had of her reminded me that she was gone. If I thought about her arms, say, reaching toward her bedside clock, my next thought was a feeling of sadness that those same arms weren't with me. I kept thinking of her, then feeling her absence, around and around in a circle of mounting frustration. I got out of the car, but even then, standing on the stable concrete sidewalk, I was still going in circles. And thank god for anger, because even though I wasn't aware of feeling it, it was acting as a stimulant. Without it I might have given up. I might have let the hopelessness of the situation defeat me. My whole inability to locate Anne, which might have led to *desperare*, instead had the opposite effect. It steeled my resolve and convinced me that my belief was the right belief, that I would be able to transform the world.

I was standing next to a bulb-headed parking meter, following my imagination around and around, trying to focus on Anne, and that's when I saw her walking along the sidewalk on the opposite side of the street.

She looked like Anne. And not only did she look like Anne, with her short, dark hair, but she walked like Anne. And not just a little either. I recognized, when she stood, the way she was standing. She was standing across the street, on the sunny side of the street, looking in the window of a store. I crossed the street, walking toward her, and when I got to her she seemed to be looking at the images of mannequins in bathing suits inside the store window. But she must've been looking at her own reflection on the surface of the window, and she must have seen *my* reflection, because when I got to about an arm's length from the back of her black hair she turned around.

42

"You're not Anne," I blurted out.

"Who are you?"

"I'm sorry," I said. "I thought you were someone else." She looked about as close as you could look to Anne without actually being Anne, and because there wasn't much to say, I smiled. Or tried to. And she tried to smile, possibly, but seemed unable to. So she swallowed. Then I swallowed. And there was nothing to be afraid of, really, but for some reason I started talking, either because she looked like Anne, or because I *thought* she looked like Anne, or because I needed a sense of protection. I felt that by talking I had some protection, and if I kept talking the thing that was protecting me would stay in place.

"You really look like this other person," I said.

I stood there in front of the window display, talking, not about any specific subject, just talking, as if there was something I was saying, as if by saying anything, anything could be said, because even if that were so, even if by standing and, in a normal tone of voice . . . not that I didn't feel strongly about what I was saying, because I did, but what I was saying . . . I forgot what I was saying. But I kept going on because my heart was pounding, that's the expression, pounding. Inside my chest. I wanted to be calm, to be like the sea, but I wasn't. I was shivering. I wanted to say some comprehensible words but the words were frozen in my frozen mouth, and my mind, that was also frozen, literally, unable to think, even to the next moment. She was standing there perfectly still, not speaking, head slightly tilted, watching my lips moving and moving until, after a while, I ran out of words. Or the words ran out of meaning. And my stomach. I could feel my stomach telling me something. My stomach was telling me that something was not quite right.

This person in front of me wasn't who I wanted her to be.

I wanted to find Anne, or the scent of Anne, hidden somewhere in or on this person. But there wasn't any Anne. I could feel the old despair imploding inside me, and I wanted a glass of water. But there wasn't any water.

I stepped closer.

The first principle of transformation is to move so gradually that nothing seems to happen until—without having created any resistance—it's already happened. And that's what I did. I gradually moved closer until I was close enough to see the hairs on her face. I could see the tension in the muscles of her cheeks, and her lips, which were taut, and the skin of her face looked as if it covered the face of a skull.

The second principle of transformation is to do the thing you're compelled to do, and I felt compelled to do something, so I reached out. I didn't think about it, but I saw myself as I reached out my hand, slowly, and touched this person, lightly, just below the cheek.

I expected the muscles of her face to go limp and relaxed, and her lips and the muscles around her lips to become full and relaxed, and her shoulders to relax. But that didn't happen.

She just looked at me. And then she walked away.

2

I wasn't keeping track of the mileage because the mileage didn't matter. What mattered to me were the clues, and so I concentrated my intuition, unsuccessfully, on looking for clues. And lack of success is exhausting, and after a day without success, my intuition needed some rest, so I pulled off the road into the town of Charleston, West Virginia. It was the state capital, a town with brick buildings and people crossing streets.

I parked by a newsstand, bought a *New York Times*, and got some change. I needed the quarters because, even without my cell phone, I was calling my house at regular intervals. I found a pay phone in front of a diner and listened to the ringing, half hoping that what I knew was happening wasn't happening. That Anne would pick up. I was wishing this unnecessary nightmare would just stop. But it didn't. I got the same answer I always got. Silence. No Anne. No clue. And I wanted to smash the receiver into the stupid box that seemed, at the moment, to be the cause of my frustration.

Instead I called Anne's mother's house. When I did I could tell from the tone of the voice on the answering machine that the family was upset. It was a new message, with a new ending, a stoic "We're all right." And I thought, Why would they say that they're all right unless they weren't all right? Unless Anne hadn't told them where she was going. I also called some mutual friends and listened to their recorded voices for a sign that Anne had appeared. She hadn't. I checked the obituary section of the newspaper, not that I would have believed anything anyway. There were a million different versions of the truth, and I wanted my own particular version.

In an effort to facilitate the creation of that version, I crossed the street to the plain glass windows of a barber college. Not a barber university, but a college, for haircutting, and I opened the glass door and a long row of barber chairs was on the left, a long mirror on the right, or vice versa. Anyway, a number of young men and old men were standing by the chairs. As I entered, a woman at a metal desk asked me what I wanted, meaning what kind of cut, and also if I wanted a shave. Well, I thought I probably did need a haircut, but I usually cut my own hair, and usually I shaved myself as well, but I told the woman that I wanted a shave. I paid the two dollars and she handed me a stub and I went to chair number three and sat. A soft, round-headed man elegantly unfurled a white sheet, cascaded it over my chest, and as I leaned back into the chair, for the first time since I'd left New York I let myself begin to relax.

There may have been music playing, but what I remember were the cushions of the chair and the minty breath of the man, his voice surrounding me, talking about something, soothing and low, and his hands, warm and smooth, touching my cheek and neck, relaxing the tightened muscles, and I could have slept, but it was better than sleeping. And then the towel. A hot white towel was placed delicately over my face, and in the darkness I could see nothing, and I wanted to see nothing and think nothing, just nothing. No me, no Anne, no fear, sadness . . . nothing. I imagined my whiskers, such as they were, softening, and the man's voice asking me some questions, and for me there was only one question. I told the man what I was doing. I told him about my wife. I said she'd run away. I talked about my dream of finding her. Under the white sheet I told him my

46

dream and incubated the dream, and his voice seemed to moan or hum or drawl understandingly.

Then the warm towel was pulled from my face, and I realized that the man who'd covered me with the towel was no longer there, that he'd been replaced by a younger man, not a younger version of the original barber, but by a different barber entirely. The sweet eucalyptus smell was the same, but I knew by his touch that a switch had occurred. The hands, when they touched my face, didn't soothe and caress but merely applied whatever substance was meant to be applied, in this case, shaving cream, and I wouldn't say it didn't feel good, but not in the way I'd felt before. This new man, or young man, was doing his job, but without passion, and as I sat there I wasn't sure which of the two barbers I'd told my story to.

So I said to the new barber standing behind me, "What do you think?"

He said something about the work at hand, something like "Easy does it," or "We'll have you ready in no time," something that an experienced man might say but that he was saying in order to seem experienced, and yet because he wasn't experienced and hadn't lived enough to be experienced, it wasn't right. And I noticed then that I was starting to get a little annoyed at this younger barber.

"I asked you what you thought," I said.

And as I sat in the still soft cushions the young man told me what he thought. He said he thought I was joking. He thought it must be a joke, he said, "a hopeless joke," to look for someone in the whole expanse of the whole entire country. And whether or not he intended me to hear the disdain in his voice, or feel the humiliation, it didn't really matter. Gradually the comfortable cushions became not so comfortable, and the hot lather not so soothing, and the voice, which had never been that mellifluous, became grating and sour and I wanted to get up. I felt an impulse to move, but because by this time the barber had unsheathed the straight-edged tool of his trade—his razor—and was scraping it across my skin, I *couldn't* move. And the fact that I couldn't move made the impulse to do so more pronounced.

Although the agitation I felt was centered in my chest, the thing I was hating was this barber. As the straight-edged razor slid or scraped its way across my neck I felt betrayed. I was mad at the first barber for leaving me with this guy because he was touching my face. And I hated it. I sat perfectly still on the outside, but inside I was churning. All I could think of was moving and the necessity of moving, but because of the razor next to my neck I couldn't.

In thinking about moving, however, I was preparing myself for the prophecy that would ultimately fulfill itself. Sitting in the chair, the sheet spread over my chest and shoulders, I'd planted the seed of moving, and although I thought I had it under control, before I knew what I was doing, that's when my face was cut. Just barely. Not the barber's fault. He wasn't being a bad barber. I just happened to twitch, slightly, and the uniform surface across which the blade had been cutting was suddenly not uniform. It changed direction, or I changed direction. And although it was more of a nick than a cut, it didn't matter. It wasn't what the barber had *done*, it was what he had *said*. An impossibility, he'd said. Hopeless, he'd said, referring to my attempt to find Anne. He was wrong, but he'd said it.

And when he whisked away the white sheet, smiled politely, and indicated that I should rise, I wasn't ready to rise. There's something called "dealing with anger," and yes, I'd been angry plenty of times, but I wasn't especially skilled at dealing with the feeling. It always seemed a little dangerous. But it was preferable to the fear that he might be right. And so I was mad, and I knew I was mad because, although I still felt obligated to tip this guy, when I stood up from his chair and reached into my pocket I started feeling for something insignificant, some coin with which I would show him my displeasure. But since I'd used all my coins for the telephone, I pulled out instead a wad of folded dollar bills, and the bill on the outside had writing, in blue ink, "I ❤ Victor." This was the bill I handed to the barber, not thanking him, just handing it, hoping he would understand what he'd done, hoping he would feel ashamed and penitent, but of course instead of looking at the bill, he just took it, stuck it in his pocket and turned to his waiting chair.

3

It was easy enough to dismiss the opinion of a barber by classifying him as an idiot. He might have been an idiot or he might have been a savant, it didn't matter because what he'd said had been untenable. I knew where Anne was going, and the idea that I should give up hope of finding her was . . . I wouldn't even say the words, even in my head. Negative thoughts would drain my confidence, and I needed my confidence, and was trying to stop any leak of any confidence I had. And yet I could feel it ebbing away. Replaced by doubt. And doubt wasn't good. I wanted to be honest and admit the complexity of what was happening, but I refused to doubt my project.

I was determined not to succumb. And what enabled me not to succumb was anger. Until now the anger had been camouflaged by other emotions but now it was beginning to show itself, creeping out from the shadows and attaching itself to the objects of my world.

My car, for instance.

I liked the car and I trusted the car, but it wasn't completely perfect. First of all, it wasn't made for someone more than six feet tall. Even with the seat in a semireclining position my head rubbed up against the brushed-velvet roof. And because I was constantly in a semireclining position, my neck was aching from the strain of holding up my head. Also the radio reception was almost nonexistent, and although I'd brought along a few tapes, the tape player didn't seem to work anymore. Also, the engine sounded like the keening of an agonized child. I knew these were minor inconveniences, outweighed by the usefulness of the car and my feeling of partnership with the car, but still I felt betrayed.

And then the car didn't start.

I was standing on a commercial street, with decorations on the light poles, looking into the open hood of the Pulsar, jiggling the wires connecting the battery to the rest of the engine, hoping something would happen. And when nothing did, I kept trying, listening to the sound it made as it almost started but didn't. I tried to will it to start. I knew where the spark plugs were and pushed them deeper into their sockets. I felt the belts and looked for what they call the starter, assuming the problem was related to that. I did everything a nonmechanic might think to do. I hit various parts of the engine with a screwdriver, and then I tried the car again, hoping that my luck or my desire or my desperation would somehow change what was happening. And when it didn't, I wanted to hit the car, but since I needed the car, the only thing I could think of hitting was myself. I imagined placing the tip of a large gun next to my temple and blowing a hole through my head.

That's when I saw this person walking in my direction. I wasn't parked that far from the highway, where apparently this guy had been standing, not quite *on* the highway because that was illegal, but standing at the place where Charleston ended. He walked over and joined me at the fender. He was wearing a blue watchcap.

"May I help you?" I said.

"What's the problem?" he said, and he looked under the oily hood at the oily pieces of engine. He braced his hand on the radiator, reached in, jiggled a few wires, and told me to give it another try. He had a wispy virginal beard and smelled of patchouli. I told him I'd already given it a try, but this didn't seem to worry him. He said something about giving the car some time.

"Time for what?" I said.

"It's a car," he said, as if that was an explanation.

"Yes," I said, "and it's a car that's not running."

He told me again to try it, and because he seemed so sure of himself I got in the car, and when I turned the ignition the car miraculously started. It seemed miraculous to me anyway, so when this man, whose name was Alex, asked if he could have a ride I asked where he was going. "Lexington," he said, and immediately I cleared away the various maps and boxes from the passenger seat to make space for him to sit. Which he did.

Now things were ticking. I felt that my mind, the unconscious part of it, knew what was happening. Without quite knowing why, I became convinced that by giving him a ride I would relieve some of the pressure I was feeling. And by pressure I mean the sense of failure that was lodging itself in my upper chest.

By sense of failure I mean the disconnect between the world I wanted and the world as it was. I saw Alex as a bridge, both a bridge and a compass, and by compass I mean a part of the natural world that would tell me where to go. Try as I might to become part of the natural world, I was separated from it, and I thought Alex, with his army-green backpack, his worn-down running shoes, and his home in Kentucky, would have access to parts of the world unknown to me, such as where Anne was.

He was going home, he said, and as we drove through the Appalachian hills I briefly recounted my experience at the gas station in New Jersey. Even without hearing the whole story, Alex seemed to understand. He told me to let it go. He said that trying to contain it would only give it power, and what I ought to do, he said, a more effective approach, would be to admit it exists, allow it to exist. "Let it out and see where it goes."

"By 'it' you mean . . . ?"

"Take it off of yourself and put it into the world," he said. "It won't go away if you keep pushing it away." Trying to get rid of it, he said, was just another way of holding on to it.

I still wasn't sure what the "it" was we were talking about, but that was all right. I was content at that point, happy for something that wasn't the wavering radio, or the hissing tape player, and this guy's voice, whatever he was talking about, was soothing and tranquil.

And so we drove, taking periodic gas stops and pee breaks, and part of the regimen during these breaks included a dose of yoga. He was religious about his yoga, which is why, when we stopped at a roadside Kuntry Kitchen restaurant, while we were sitting at a table by the window waiting for the check, Alex slid out of the bench seat, stretched out on the smooth blue carpeting, and began a series of salutations to the sun.

This particular action might have been typical in an ashram somewhere, but it was atypical in this particular restaurant, and a woman at a nearby table, an older woman facing Alex, puffing away on a long thin cigarette, began shaking her head. Alex couldn't see it because he was involved in his posture, but I saw the woman, and I mention it because, although what she'd done was nothing out of the ordinary—a simple shake of the head— I felt as if she'd reached across the several tables separating us and grabbed my heart in her fist. She'd reached *through* my chest, into its beating muscle, and I could feel a pressure building up in my body and directed at this woman for imposing her judgment on another member of the human race who happened to have a different set of beliefs.

53

That's how I saw it anyway.

And the odd thing was, that although she wasn't shaking her head at *me*, I was the one who felt the pressure. And so, following Alex's earlier advice, I stood up and walked to her booth. I hadn't rehearsed what I was going to say, but concentrated on just letting it out. Let it out, I thought, and I said to her, "Is there a problem?" That's when I noticed, sitting across from the woman, her husband, or a man taking the role of husband, strong and big-bellied, and although my question was mostly rhetorical, the man was saying that there *was* a problem. And I said, "Well, why don't we look at the problem a little closer, because I think it might be *your* problem." At which point he stood up, or tried to, but because he was near the window side of the booth—and also because of his belly—he couldn't stand up that easily.

And I'm not saying I didn't have any judgments because I had plenty, and I knew it, but I wasn't concerned with noticing those judgments because I was more concerned with acting on them, with making these particular people experience a suitable form of punishment.

I wanted to be mad at something. And this is it, I thought, meaning this is the experience of anxiety turning into excitement. Instead of directing the pressure of that anxiety at myself, I had gotten it off myself and was aiming it at something in the world. And I liked it.

So there we were, the woman sitting, the man half standing, and me. And of course no sudden wave of understanding washed over the table, and in fact both of us, or all three of us, were trying, in our looks, to belittle and intimidate the other. I wanted the man to back down, and I wanted the woman to retract, not just her look, but her judgment.

Although her judgment hadn't bothered Alex—who blithely

continued his salutations—it bothered me. And although the couple eventually left without incident, it continued to bother me. I couldn't get that lady, or some residue of that lady, out of my body. She was stuck inside my body, burned into my body's memory, and I was unable or unwilling to leave her behind. As I walked back to the car I was still feeling, in my stomach and chest, the incipient rage that for a moment had been directed at something other than me, and was now back *in* me, submerged inside the shell I had come to call myself.

4

We spent the night in a rest area, Alex in the car and me, nestled in my sleeping bag, on a grassy area next to the car. The diesel engines of the big trucks rumbled all night, and the high-voltage illumination, meant to prevent crime, prevented me from sleeping. On the one hand I thought I *should* sleep, and on the other I was still imagining retributions for the lady back at the restaurant.

The next morning I was walking out of the cinder-block bathroom when Alex, practicing his yoga on the grass, suggested I take off my shoes and join him. I was willing enough to touch my toes if I could, but before I did, while I was lining up my feet, he tapped my chest and told me to let the air out. He told me to relax my shoulders and take a deep cleansing breath, and because I was used to following instructions I was about to follow his. But I didn't want to take a cleansing breath. A deep cleansing breath might have alleviated the symptoms I was feeling, but I didn't mind the symptoms.

Thank god for anger, I thought. Although I didn't know what it was protecting me from exactly, I could tell it was giving me a chance to feel something other than loss. In that sense it was good, if not necessarily pleasant. Compared with loss or sorrow, anger was a balm, and rather than let it go, I wanted to perpetuate it. And when Alex started talking about Anne I had my opportunity.

He suggested, matter-of-factly, that maybe my wife *wanted*

to disappear, that maybe she preferred *not* to be found. He'd seen the photo on the dashboard and I'd told him a more complete version of the dark car at the gas station, and the brakes screeching, and then Anne disappearing. And now he was saying, "She probably needs some space. A little time away," he said. And although he didn't laugh when he said it, or even smile, I told him I wasn't joking. He said that he knew I wasn't joking, that he didn't mean it as a joke, but by then it didn't matter.

Maybe I didn't like his cavalier manner, or maybe I had a problem with his presumption. Or maybe I hated the idea that what he'd said was possibly right. Which it wasn't.

But as I say, it didn't matter.

Since I'd already taken the step of identifying with the sensation of anger, the next step was feeling its discomfort, and the step after that was to get rid of it.

"What I mean," he said, "is that I think it might take some time, but I do believe, eventually, that you'll find your wife." I knew he was trying to apologize, but by then I already had my excuse, a reason to place my discomfort onto something else.

So I got mad. And because I was mad I did several things. First, I just tried ignoring him. And when that didn't do anything, the next thing I did, after we got in the car and started driving, was, I tried to hypnotize him. In college I'd studied hypnosis and so I started talking to him, saying things like "Are you getting sleepy?" and "How do you know if you know you're sleeping when you're looking out the window and seeing that sleep are grazing in the fields?" Things like that.

I'd heard about the concept of releasing your anger, and that's what I was trying to do. I thought I was getting it off my chest and that by doing so I would feel better. Except I didn't. It was still there, wrapped around my heart, a definite impulse to somehow hurt Alex. At the same time I could see that he hadn't done anything really. He was probably a student, someone who wanted to be friendly, and was, in fact, willing to express an opinion in a friendly way. But it was already too late. I had already enveloped myself in a skin of anger, enclosed myself within the protection of this skin, and as we drove along I wasn't speaking, and because the engine was loud, and because I was encased in this skin, if he said anything to me I didn't hear what it was.

We were driving along the smoothly flowing interstate, through a layer of mist in a valley, and he was saying some-thing, but I was unable or unwilling to hear what it was until he began commenting on my old maroon car, casually mentioning that, while he wasn't totally sure, he was pretty sure he'd seen a plum-colored car back at the rest area, a station wagon, and he knew there must be a million station wagons painted in some shade of red, but . . .

That was enough for me. Even the slightest hint of Anne would have been enough, and I immediately turned around. I should say I wanted to turn around, but because we were driving on a divided interstate highway there was no opportunity to turn around. There was no exit. It was one-way as far as we could see and I kept driving, for miles, expecting to come to an off-ramp or a turnoff, and mile after mile of trees and more trees but no turnoffs. I was mad at Alex and mad at myself and mad at the interstate highway commission. It was doubly frustrating because I could see, just across the grassy median, the road I wanted.

But I couldn't *get* to that road. I was separated from that road or the direction the road implied, waiting for an exit, hoping an exit would suddenly appear, and when none did, I started to go slightly crazy. I was already in the left-hand lane, and when I couldn't stand the frustration any longer, I veered farther left, off the highway and onto the asphalt part of the median. Alex was holding on to the dashboard as I started driving down the bumpy grass slope, and it *was* bumpy, so I drove slowly, down one side, and carefully, at an angle, across the gully and then up the other side. I was heading in the opposite direction now, waiting at the border of the grass for a chance to pull into the traffic flow when, just as that chance was about to present itself, a car pulled up, a state trooper car with a flashing light. It stopped in front of my car, blocking access to the highway, and a man with high boots walked over.

I tried to explain to him that this wasn't a very good time. "I'm sorry," I said, and I told him that I knew I'd committed a traffic violation but that I was in the middle of an emergency. I tried to reason with the man, to placate his desire to enforce the law, but that wasn't good enough. It seemed this particular trooper was either a tough guy, or acting like a tough guy, and when he told me to get out of the car that's when the struggle really started.

I wanted to decide what was going to happen, and the trooper also wanted to decide what would happen, and initiated by some comment—or some nonverbal aspect of that comment— I felt myself pushed to the point where the choices in my mind were reduced to either surrendering to this unjust power or doing something stupid. And what I did was, I held my hand in the shape of a gun—index finger forward, thumb pointing up—and I pretended to aim this imaginary gun at the trooper, who with unexpected force threw me against the side of my car and locked my wrists in handcuffs.

And I say thank god for anger because although it's good for giving a sense of protection, it's also good for changing things, or breaking through things. The power struggle had now become physical, and even though I was bound by the hand-cuffs I was ready to *get* physical. Alex, still sitting in the car, was peacefully trying to explain the situation, but the trooper wasn't listening. It was *his* situation and *his* control, and since anger is a by-product of lack of control, and since I had nothing if not lack of control, the anger that had been smoldering in me started burning. Even with my face pressed into the metal of the squad car, the adrenaline flowing in my blood felt liberating. Of course when I attempted to enact that liberation by pulling my hands apart I only pulled the handcuffs tighter, and while my liberation was in this way thwarted, my anger wasn't.

And again, I didn't think about what I did next, I just started doing it. I suddenly started jerking around, spasmodically twisting my body until I fell onto the asphalt, writhing in what I didn't even know, just writhing, like what I imagine someone having a fit would do, a physical seizure, and I could tell the man was dumbfounded. I was shaking my head, letting the spittle spill from my mouth, and I could hear him tell me I'd better not be faking it. He said he was going to take me to some jail and I'd be butt-fucked by certain inmates at this particular jail. So I kept writhing.

Alex, at this point, kneeled over me, and I wanted to signal to him that I was fine, but because the trooper was watching I had to keep writhing, surreptitiously winking at Alex, who kept asking me if I was all right. I tried to let him know that I was, but I didn't stop writhing.

Until the trooper pulled from his car a first-aid kit. He took out some smelling salts and he cracked open two candy-sized cartridges and jammed them up my nostrils. Smelling salts are supposed to be wafted *near* the nose, but he stuck them *into* my nose. And so, as my writhing subsided, I lay there, breathing through my clenched mouth. I could hear Alex somewhere over my head admonishing me to "keep breathing, keep breathing," and what a stupid thing to say, I thought. Of course I'm breathing.

How can I not keep breathing? But in thinking what a stupid thing it was, I momentarily took my mind off the trooper. Momentarily my anger ran out of fuel. And at that point I could have added some fuel, could have fanned the flames of the struggle I was having, and the thing that changed was the realization of what I was struggling for.

I started thinking about Anne.

I sat up and looked at the patrolman. He was just a person, no worse than anybody else. He had the rounded shoulders of a man past his physical prime, and I could see how he might've felt threatened, somewhat, by my aggressive gesture. I offered a conciliatory remark, like "I'm sorry if I freaked you out" or "I got a little excited," and we started talking. He took the broken pellets out of my nose. Still cuffed, I told him about Anne, and about why I was seeming so desperate, and he must have had a sympathetic streak. He indicated his understanding of my predicament by tying it into the passion he had for fly fishing. I could see he was attempting a rapprochement, and as we talked, the anger, which had seemed so liberating a moment ago, now seemed, in light of my desire to be with Anne, not very helpful. So I held it in. For Anne's sake. I listened to his fly-fishing monologue, nodding at appropriate times, and in this way I created—or *we* created—a sense of fellow feeling. We were getting along, finding our commonality, and after about a half hour of this relational negotiation he unlocked the handcuffs, gave me a warning, and then he let us drive away.

5

Your arms. They're my favorite parts of your body, from the wrist bone up through the fine hairs of your forearm, the loose skin inside your elbow, to the taut flexors and extensors of your upper arm, turning gently into shoulder and collarbone and neck. There are certain sleeveless shirts you wear, and when you do I feel like taking those arms, like autonomous entities, holding them above your head, and running my nose down their entire velvet length. I would melt into those arms if I could, but instead I do the closest thing, kissing the delicate skin of your biceps, taking into my mouth the whole fibrous mass of muscle under your skin. Because you're strong, and because you see yourself as strong, you like to do things. You like rock climbing. We both do. We aren't experts, but I remember one night, riding on our bikes in the wind to a health club in midtown with a faux rock wall where people practice their ascents. You're wearing a tank top and bicycle shorts and we rent the special shoes and helmets and we've been climbing for about an hour, noticing among the climbers one blond man, without companion or rope, climbing like a muscular spider along the artificial notches and grooves that signify handholds of actual rock. When we finish, sitting at a table in the health club drinking some healthy drink, the man we've been watching walks up to us. He introduces himself as an Austrian mountain climber and shows us a book, a large book with photographs of him climbing various European rock faces, famous ones, he assures us. His accent is engaging and he offers to give us some pointers, a generous thing, except that during the whole conversation, I have the impression that he's talking only to you. He's looking at me but I can't help noticing that his body is tilted toward you. And you're turned toward him, listening to him, taking him in. After we get home, lying in bed that night, I can tell there's something between us. I assume it's that Austrian fucker, or your Austrian desire for him rather than me, and when we *do* make love I can feel a palpable barrier separating us. Your mind is elsewhere. And of course you assure me that the Austrian man means nothing to you, all the typical things a person might say, but I know, or think I know, that you're not telling me everything. And maybe he *is* better than I am, stronger and kinder and more understanding than I could ever be. But he isn't that handsome, not in my opinion. You, however, don't agree with my opinion, and I see this unwillingness to take my side as a kind of betrayal. I see it and feel it, and it feels like a knife cutting us apart. I call it jealousy because jealousy is a famous emotion, but I could do something to change it. Attention is what you want and I could easily give you that attention. I could understand, or try to understand, but I want attention too. And I don't want to compete for it. Not with him. You've taken a solemn vow, we both have, and I can't tell if I'm sad or mad, and maybe I'm both because a gap opens up, like a wedge driven between us, and as this wedge slowly pries us apart, a hundred disparate emotions combine in me to create a sense of disorientation that never completely goes away.

Driving with Alex through West Virginia, inspecting the various clapboard towns for my old maroon station wagon, I was still feeling that disorientation, or something like it. My job was to find Anne, and in order to do that I needed my awareness focused on the world, and because this disorientation was clouding that focus, to cure myself I pulled off the highway somewhere in Kentucky.

I found a small road which led eventually to a parking lot for an overpriced tourist attraction, an underground cavern or cave. Instead of visiting the cave, we got out of the car, peed in the trees, and decided to walk down the hill from the parking lot. We followed a single-track trail that led through a pine tree forest that ended at a small round pond with a steep bank and frogs making noise. It was surrounded by birch trees and maple trees, and the good old maple trees reminded me of our garden. Which reminded me of Anne. Which reminded me of my disorientation—like the hand of the woman in the restaurant—attaching itself to my heart.

"Aren't you coming in?" Alex said.

I sat on the grass slope at the edge of the pond watching him take his clothes off. I shook my head.

"Why not?" he said. "It would do you good."

"Oh really?" I said, thinking that he didn't know who I was, and that swimming in a slimy pond wouldn't do anything any good.

He reminded me that he'd fixed the car. "Remember the car?" he said.

"I'm not a car," I told him.

"Your body is a vehicle," he said. And then he jumped. He was standing at the high point of the bank, completely naked, looking into the water, and then, feet first, arms flailing, he jumped into the water. He splashed and hooted from the middle of the pond, and although the water was obviously cold, he seemed to be enjoying it.

I stayed rooted where I was, dressed and warm, and when he climbed out of the water with a huge smile on his face I made a point of looking away. Birds may have been singing peacefully in the trees but I wasn't listening.

"It's not that bad," he said.

I made some disparaging face.

"It's only cold in comparison to out here," he said.

"Which is where I am," I said. "Out here." I told him I was perfectly fine.

"If that's what you think you need," he said, and he walked again to the edge of the bank and again he jumped into the water. I watched him breaststroking his way across the pond.

I'd been fairly successful at protecting myself, and the reason I decided at that moment to step out of the skin of that protection was . . . I don't know what it was, but I took my clothes off. I stood naked on the grassy bank. Alex yelled to me to jump, and I was trying to get ready to do that. "Jump," he said, but there was the thought of the freezing water and the warmth I'd be giving up. That was on one side. On the other was something in me, something I needed to cleanse myself of, and I thought . . . or rather, for a moment I didn't think. I just jumped.

Actually I dove. He'd said it was deep enough so I dove in, head first. And it *was* freezing. He said it wasn't that bad, but it was that bad. I also started hooting. We were both kicking furiously to adjust to the cold or to counteract the cold, but I think the fact that it was freezing, the fact that the cold itself cleared away all other thoughts and sensations, made us happy. I say we were happy because both of us were smiling.

I stayed in only a few seconds, and then we were both on the bank, running in place and flapping our arms to keep warm. We were two naked hyperventilating apes, laughing at the exhilaration of pure sensation. When our thoughts, slowly, started coming back we put on our pants. I was drying myself with my T-shirt when Alex, apropos of nothing apparent, turned to me.

He was shivering and he looked at me, and he waited until I looked directly at him. We stopped running in place.

"I'm sorry," he said.

I could see the goose bumps covering his body. I nodded.

We were face-to-face in a way we hadn't been able to be in the car, and why at that moment I don't know, but that's when it hit me. Anne. The fear of losing her. I don't know if Alex *saw* the fear, but I know that I was feeling it. That I would never see Anne again. That my life, and everything I'd based my life on, had gone. That I'd never get it back. And at this point, something in me started welling up—and it didn't matter about Alex. I was staring into his face but I wasn't seeing him or thinking about him.

The thing I'd been successfully holding in me, or keeping out of me, was gathering in my chest or belly. And when I let my attention go there, when I let myself experience what it was, it came up from down in my body, through my chest, and the sobs just came, in waves, the tears flowing from the corners of my eyes, mixing with the pond water dripping down my face. And once they started coming they kept coming, and I stood there, unworried about the strange face I was probably making, feeling the peristaltic convulsions come, not making them come, just feeling the empty space from where they seemed to originate.

And when they finally subsided, when whatever spasm it was died down, I stood, staring into the pond and shivering. We both were shivering. And then, without speaking, we got dressed. Slightly damp and still shivering, we got in the car, and with the heat turned up, we drove out of the hill country and on toward Lexington.

6

We arrived in the late afternoon. Alex navigated us to a bar, an Irish bar (or faux Irish bar) where at that moment a girls' softball team was celebrating some local victory. I was still a little chilled, and because I didn't know anyone, I sat at a table near the jukebox wall, removed from the locus of the festivities.

I noticed Alex circulate among the crowd, bowing imperceptibly when he met his friends, bowing, ordering beer, and talking to a girl in a ponytail. I noticed her several times that night but never spoke to her—she never came to my table—and after a while, after the beer and the infectious celebratory mood wore off, I drove Alex to the place where he lived, a cedar-shingled house on a quiet street with lawns and large trees. Inside, because there wasn't a lot of furniture, we sat on the hardwood floor, drinking leftover red wine, and because there was no sofa I assumed I'd be sleeping on the floor. I had it all laid out in my mind. With a few rugs stacked on top of each other I'd have a mattress, soft enough for sleep. I went to the car, brought in my sleeping bag, and as I was spreading it out on a rug beneath a painted bookcase, the girl from the Irish tavern walked into the room. Alex hadn't mentioned it, but it turned out that she was his roommate.

She joined us, sitting cross-legged on the wood floor, a bowl of miniature carrots between us, and she was wearing an oversized T-shirt and what seemed like the bottom of a bathing suit. Although a lot of her skin was visible, I had the impression that she wasn't showing off, that this was how she walked around, and she was determined to do the same thing, even if a strange or unknown man was camped out in her living room.

Laura was her name, and when Alex retired to his room Laura and I started talking. She said she was a cartoonist, and so we talked, not about cartoons, but about the philosophical foundation of animation. About how you start with a point, and then you have another point, and between them you have a line, and by moving the line just slightly, just imperceptibly moving the line over and over and over, over time, you begin to effect a change. You start to tell a story.

She started out asking some innocuous question about where I was from, which led to something and then to something else, and at a certain point in the conversation she commented on the solidity of the floor and the discomfort of sleeping on the hard wood surface, and not too long after that she invited me to sleep in her bed. Not *with* her, but in her bed. At first I told her it didn't matter, that I'd be fine on the floor, but I realized I was saying it just to be polite, and why should I be that? Her bed, she said, was large enough, and her offer seemed sincere, an offer of kindness. So I told her, Why not? I didn't say the words "Why not?" I just said, "Yes, I would love to sleep on a bed."

She was wearing the same large T-shirt on the bed; the bathing suit, it turned out, was ordinary regular-sized underwear. And there we lay, on our backs, in parallel lines. I was facing the ceiling, making a point of keeping my body straight, imagining an invisible border between us. I let my eyes close, and we weren't talking, not at first, and then she said something about her lack of success in the restaurant business. She was a waitress in a local restaurant and apparently she wasn't getting the shifts she wanted. We talked about her boyfriend, or ex-boyfriend, and I said something about looking for my lost wife.

She seemed to understand. We seemed—mutually, I think—to be getting along, and I didn't sleep and she didn't sleep, and as we spoke, and as I listened to the sound of the whispering human voice, I was lulled into—not a trance—but I moved closer, so that my shoulder was touching, or almost touching, her shoulder, so that only an infinitesimal gap existed between my arm and hers. Although I couldn't see her arm, I imagined it, brown and smooth and still.

At some point, under the spell of the words that were passing between us, without my actually doing anything, Laura's arm transformed itself—or I transformed it—into a different arm. I imagined Anne's arm next to me. And because a person's arm is connected to the rest of the body, gradually, in my mind, Laura herself was replaced by Anne. Not an image of Anne or a representation of Anne. The person beside me *was* Anne, and I was lying there, happily absorbing the old familiarity and warmth.

Because my eyes were closed it was easy enough to alter the body beside me, but because the voice wasn't Anne's voice, and because it wasn't possible to shut my ears, I had a little trouble keeping the audio part of the fantasy intact. But as she spoke about her plans to move to a bigger city, and as the sound of her voice traveled from her mouth through the air to my ears and then into my brain, over time, I was able to transform that voice and mold it into what I wanted. The knowledge that the voice I was hearing was a voice I was making, I let that recede, happy to usher out of consciousness any evidence of my own volition.

I was able to overlook the knowledge that she wasn't Anne, so that to me, she *was* Anne. In the back of my mind was the fear that she would say something or do something to wake me up, but because this new reality was preferable to the earlier one, I was able to maintain it. I settled into the more comfortable mode of lying with Anne, and the reality of Anne, such as it was, became more solid and stable, and when it got to the point where I was sure of its solidity, that's when she decided to go to the bathroom.

When she sat up and crawled over me, wearing her oversized T-shirt, it was Anne in an oversized T-shirt, crawling over me as she'd crawled over me a million times. That's the thing about a fantasy: once it gets started it takes on a life of its own, and I kept it alive by picturing Anne in the bathroom, sitting on the toilet and washing her hands and then climbing back into bed, which she did.

And when she did I had a million questions to ask her. Mainly I wanted to know if she loved me, and if she did, how could she leave me standing in front of a convenience store.

When she lay down on the partially made bed and resumed her position beside me, I asked her, "Where did you go?"

"The bathroom," she said.

"No, I know, but before. Where did you go?"

"Before what?" she said.

I was talking about the gas station in New Jersey, but she didn't seem to remember that, or didn't want to. So I asked her *why* she'd left.

"I had to pee."

"Not that," I said.

"Then what?" she said.

And we went around like this, in a circuit of mutual misunderstanding. And the words were only a symptom.

I was lying there in the darkness behind my eyelids, imagining Anne, and of course, if I had opened my eyes I would have seen that Anne wasn't there. But I had no desire to see that. I was thinking of Anne, wondering where she'd gone. I was hurt.

I thought she was going to be there. She said she was going to be there, that she was going to wait for me and she didn't wait for me and now I didn't know what she was doing. Or feeling. I thought we had an understanding. I certainly had an understanding, but she obviously had a different understanding because she hadn't even contacted me. What was I supposed to do? Was I even part of it, this thing that happened so suddenly? Or did she plan it all along? Some *thing* she couldn't tell me. I didn't know. How would I know? What the fuck was she doing to me? That's what I wanted to know. And there's no reason to get mad at someone you love, except the way I saw it, she wasn't being fair with me.

"I don't even know if you're alive," I said.

And at that moment the person next to me sat up and tapped my chest. "I'm here," she said. "Open your eyes."

"Open my eyes? Okay." And I opened my eyes.

Although the light was not that great, I sat up to tell her that what she was doing was wrong, wrong to me and wrong in general, and as I was about to tell her this I looked into her oval face, at her eyes, and the whites of her eyes, and of course I saw that the person I was talking to wasn't Anne.

I remembered the Irish bar, and the baby carrots, and then the fantasy vanished. I don't know what I actually said, if I even said anything, but after a while I was aware that the feeling I'd had a moment before had passed. Something had come along and taken its place. The fear was still there but the anger was gone, and I didn't know where it went, but fine, I thought. I could hold on to the anger or not, fan the flames or not. And I chose not.

I turned to Laura, and I don't know what I thought, but in the middle of thinking it she told me that my body was a vehicle. She said I could use it, or I didn't have to.

Then she lay back down on top of the covers.

Here she was, with a man, with the body of a man, and she was hoping he would be a normal man, and now she was presented with someone who was talking to her in a way that made no sense. Half naked and next to her, and what is supposed to happen now? That's what she was probably thinking.

I was propped on my elbow looking at her, trying to think of my body as a vehicle, and maybe I was aware of some galvanic skin communication in the muscles of our arms, or my arm, because it seems to me that under normal circumstances we would begin kissing. I remember thinking that I ought to be kissing this person, and I *would* have been kissing her except for one small thing. She wasn't who I wanted her to be.

So we didn't kiss.

And the lack of kissing, which I expected to wedge us apart, instead seemed to open up a kind of pathway between us. Instead of relating via the kiss, we had to relate in a different way, in a companionship way, and so we began to talk. Everyone has a story, and we had stories, and we brought our stories to this place, this bed, and we told each other as much as we wanted to be heard, or as much as we could bear.

We lay there, without speaking. And because, for a moment, I'd been with Anne, I was fairly happy. Although she wasn't Anne anymore, she *had* been, and that was enough. I think we were both fairly happy, and happily we went to sleep.

She did anyway.

I just lay in the bed, waiting for the light to come in the window, and when it did I slipped out from under the covers, packed my bags, and when Alex got up I ate cereal with him before he went to work. I liked Alex, and I hoped that when I thanked him for his navigation skills, he understood I meant more than navigation.

When Laura got up we were going to make coffee, but there wasn't any milk so we went to a coffee shop down the street. We sat in a booth and seemed to be getting along, connecting easily with each other, talking about whatever came up, just talking and talking, and we hardly noticed when we left the coffee shop. We were walking along the damp sidewalk, still talking and walking, and right about as we passed my car, which was parked on the street near her house, that's when I stopped. I couldn't go back with her to the house, I thought, because I had somewhere else to go. I realized that time was passing, and I couldn't spend whatever time there was sitting around a Lexington living room.

I had to get on the road, I told her.

She asked me why.

I tried to explain to her about Anne and what I was doing. I told her it felt as if a door was slowly closing in front of me, and that behind the door there was something I was still connected to.

"Do what you need to do," she said, briefly opening her arms.

And as I watched her arms open and then dangle there against her hips, I thought, Why couldn't that door also be here? Why did I have to go somewhere? Why couldn't I somehow see in these things here, or be connected through these things, this other thing I was looking for?

"I can't tell," she said. "Are you kidding?"

Behind her were green trees and behind them was actual sky with clouds. A car drove down the street and then the street was quiet. On a lawn nearby the grass was overgrown.

"Are you coming or not?" she said.

"I probably should be going," I said.

"Okay," she said, and she turned and started walking up the

sidewalk. As I watched her walk I told myself, This is what I have to do, meaning, This is what I feel, meaning, This is who I think I have to be.

7

As I drove around the town of Lexington, it was just me now, just my eyes and my ears and my own intuition, and to facilitate the appearance of that intuition I drove very slowly, unsure where that intuition would be coming from but trusting what I felt, and hoping I would come up with something.

Anne liked horse racing so I drove to a racetrack on the outskirts of town. I watched the horses practicing on the track, their breath steaming in the cool morning air, and then, because I felt like eating, I drove to a bar and grill. I parked the car on the street and went inside, but the grill part was closed. This was just a bar, low-ceilinged and not that glamorous, a long room, three steps down from the street, and half of its tables had chairs stacked on top of them. It smelled like dead beer, and the floor was sticky. It reminded me of a Polish tavern.

As casually as possible I sidled up to the bar and ordered—after seeing a man with a Budweiser bottle—the same thing, taking it to an empty table carved with hieroglyphs. The souvenirs on the walls were dusty. I could hear a buzzing, a high-pitched buzzing from somewhere. No one paid attention as I drank, which on the one hand was a relief and on the other was a disappointment. I might as well have not been there. Which, I said to myself, is fine. I drank my beer, glancing at the television perched at the end of the bar. In it, people were doing things and saying things, and they were all in some relationship with each other.

But not to me.

Light was coming from the street outside, through the diamond-shaped window in the door, and I walked to the door. It was locked. But it was a very simple thing to just turn the little knob of the lock and push the door open, which I did, and it opened. The morning was almost over, I could tell by the light. There was no one on the street, no cars, and since I felt like walking, I did.

I found a coffee shop and went inside. Although I'd said thank god for anger, I was saying now, Thank god it was gone. I was glad to be done with it, glad to be sitting at a counter eating a bowl of chicken-vegetable soup. It was cold enough outside so that the windows had fogged up, and I didn't notice when the man came in, but when the man sat down on the stool next to me I noticed his smell. I looked up and the man had pulled a tea bag out of his coat and was dipping it into a cup. He held it over the cup, watching it drip, and when it stopped dripping he put the used bag into a pocket of one of his coats. It wasn't that cold but he was wearing two separate coats. He must have sensed me watching him because he turned to me and looked at me and it looked as if he tried to smile. He showed me his brown teeth, several of which were missing, and kept the same expression frozen on his face. His lower lip stuck out like a shelf, as if it was cut, but it hadn't quite fallen off.

Then I noticed his stomach, which was swollen, but not from overeating. He wasn't fat. It was distended, as if something was inside of him, growing inside of him, as if, if it were possible, he was pregnant. The man saw where I was looking and before I could speak he said to me, "I can't get rid of it." He looked down at the thing he had down there and patted it.

"I'm sorry," I said.

"Why?" the man said.

"It's pretty big," I said.

"I know," the man said, and rested his hand on top of it.

"Is it painful?" I said.

"Feel," he said, smiling. "Feel it." And he swiveled on his stool. He wanted me to feel his stomach.

"I can see," I said. "That looks pretty good."

I saw no need to touch his stomach, but he wanted me to feel it. He reached out, grabbed my hand, and held it, in his. He was holding my hand and I didn't know quite what would be the appropriate thing to say, so I started explaining to the man about the neurological foundation of pain. I told him it was all in the mind. I explained that when you touch something, you have sensations, but those sensations aren't pain unless you think they are. "Thinking makes it so," I said, and I told the man he could have control. I told him that his body was a vehicle.

The man nodded, then guided my hand between the buttons of his shirt. He placed my hand against his taut, damp belly. It was moving with his breathing, up and down, and he pressed it there, or I pressed it there, against his belly, for what seemed like a long time.

And then I pulled my hand away. I slid my bowl of half-finished soup in front of him. I stood up and looked at the man, thinking the man would be looking at me, but he wasn't. He was drinking his tea. A song about sexual healing was playing on a radio. I wanted to say something to him, and finally, when he did look up, I said something like "Good luck" or "See you later." And then I walked out. I walked about a block down the street and I realized I was still feeling it. It was still there. I could still feel this person's belly on my hand.

III

Invidia

1

Just as a person who buys a new pair of shoes notices other people's shoes, so I was noticing cars. The rest of the day I spent driving around Lexington, around the public housing projects, the vacant lots, the liquor stores, and the "revitalized" downtown, watching cars and the people getting in and out of cars. The people were living their lives, or seemed to be, doing what they could do, given the circumstances they had.

My own circumstances were starting to feel used up. My intuition, which I'd been using to find Anne, or thought I'd been using, was gone. And even if I'd had a full supply, all the intuition in the world wouldn't find her if she didn't want to be found. She was the one who'd left me, and if, in fact, she didn't want me to find her, even if she was still here somewhere (which she probably wasn't), there was nothing I could do.

I realized I was going about this whole thing all wrong. I'd been trying to find this thing, and since the best way to find something is to stop looking so hard, I decided to stop looking for Anne. Let's be realistic, I thought, and I turned my attention to the most realistic thing I had, or the most salient realistic thing I had: my teeth. They were covered in a film of day-old plaque from not brushing. So after about an hour of driving I turned onto a road called Circle Road or Loop Road, driving past the motels and strip malls lining the road, looking for a drugstore. It was my habit now to scan the streets and parking lots, so I also did that, looking for something that by this time had become a little hazy in my mind. It wasn't hard to find a mall, a so-called megamall, filled with music and escalators and a big-brand drugstore. I walked into the upbeat music of the drugstore, bought some toothpaste, and when I walked back out into the parking lot at first I didn't notice it. It took me a couple of steps before I actually turned around and recognized that the maroon station wagon parked in the middle of the lot was *my* maroon station wagon.

I wasn't as excited as I expected I would be. I didn't start jumping up and down. I mean it *seemed* to be my old car, but it had a different license plate, a California license. So I sat in my faded red coupe, watching my old maroon car from a distance, feeling that modicum of hope returning. I brushed my teeth with some bottled water, nibbled on some cheese-flavored snack food, reclined in the seat, and generally spent the after-noon drifting in and out of thought with nothing happening to the car or any people connected to the car.

I was watching the shadows lengthen across the asphalt, waiting until someone came and took possession, and when someone did finally come, it wasn't a single person. A man and two women came out of a family restaurant named Michael's or Anthony's and got in the car. The man drove, and I followed him as he drove, getting back on the Circle Road or New Circle Road. I continued following the car around this Circle until they pulled into the parking lot of one of the many motels, this one a two-story model with a wagon wheel as part of the signage. I watched my old maroon car pull up beside another, larger car, a more luxurious car, a Mercedes or Lexus or BMW. This, I thought, made sense. Although it wasn't silver like the luxury car I remembered from New Jersey, it wasn't exactly black either. It was a kind of dark, dark gray, and I realized that my memory of the car at the gas pump might be faulty. And not just the car.

I was watching the people *inside* the car, and when they got out of the car, by this time, I'd picked out one of the people, a woman. The man and the other woman seemed somehow aligned, and the one woman seemed slightly removed, and it was this woman, the removed woman, who, whether consciously or not, I took as the primary focus of my watching. It was her I watched as she walked up the stairs—as all three of them walked up the outdoor stairs—and entered a room on the second floor.

I walked to the check-in office, past the ice machine and illuminated vacancy part of the no vacancy sign, and at the reception desk I got a room for the night. It was from this room, with its queen-sized bed and lamp and television on a table, that I looked out through the curtains to the parking lot. I was on the ground floor, not exactly below, but somewhere below, the people I now seemed to be stalking.

This was the first time I'd had a bed to myself since leaving New York, and I wanted to lie down. I needed in fact to lie down and sleep, to stretch out and relax, but I couldn't afford to relax. When they say that the joy of a motel room is also its heartbreak, they mean that since every room is basically the same, the experience of any individual room depends on the mind of the inhabitant. If there's an inclination in the lodger for comfort, then there's comfort, and if the room is not quite right, if something is wrong or missing—for me, something was missing—the room is a reminder, more than a reminder; it's a sharp stick digging into the heartache that's already there. Which was why I couldn't fall asleep. I was worried about losing the fragile thread connecting me to my old life. I saw the car, my old maroon car, as a thread or string, connected to a kite, and I was holding on, but the kite had a mind of its own.

In the morning, when I looked out to the parking lot, I saw that one of the two cars—it was a Mercedes—was gone. I threw on my shoes and walked out to the car that was still there, the station wagon. Standing under a cloudless sky, I examined it for signs of familiarity and remembered experience, and the funny thing was, I couldn't find any. There were no familiar dents or scratches. When I looked inside, there was no distinguishing crack or tear or cigarette burn to mark it as anything other than an old car, like any other old car.

The doors were locked, and walking around the car I was trying to smell some smell that might be emanating from inside. Anne had given the car a nickname, Chaucer, which came from Chaser, which came from the fact that the car was a Mercury Tracer. I was looking at the car, thinking of two possibilities. Either it was a different car—and if it was a different car then that was the end of it—or else it wasn't a different car, and these people had either bought it or stolen it, and possibly stolen Anne.

Looking through the shatterproof glass I half hoped that Anne might be hidden under the blankets in the back, that I could call in through the glass, softly, but loud enough, so that if she was tied down under the blankets she would hear me.

"Anne," I called out. "Anne."

And that's when the girl, the one I'd been watching, walked up to me. Standing slightly behind me, she said to me, in a loud whisper, "Are you interested in the car?"

As I turned, I could feel the adrenaline rushing into my bloodstream. I noticed she was wearing a blue beret.

"Who's Anne?" she says.

"I was looking at your car."

"To buy?" she says.

"Where did you get it?"

"It's not mine," she tells me. "But if you want to talk to the owner . . ." and she begins looking in her bag for a pen.

84

I touch my nonexistent breast pockets to indicate my lack of writing implement, and then she says, "Follow me." She starts walking and I follow her, back to the motel building and up the stairs to the door of her room. Where she stops. She unlocks the door and stands, wondering, I suppose, whether to let me in. I squint in through the slightly opened door, looking for clues.

"Do you like your room?" I say.

"The room?" she says, and she steps aside so that I can see inside. And I do. The room seems normal enough, and as I'm peering in she asks me if I'm looking for something.

"No," I say. "No. Just looking."

She says her name is Linda.

"That's pretty," I say.

"Thank you," she says.

"I mean it *means* pretty. In Spanish."

"Oh . . ."

"Leenda. Is how you would say it."

At that, or just after that, she invites me in. Her gestures are direct and forthright and I follow her into her room, an exact replica of my own room except with more clothes hanging on the chairs. As she roots around for a pen and paper I'm watching her, and I notice a lightness in her movements, and in those movements I detect a kind of contentment or happiness. She seems to be at ease. And it's exactly this ease or contentment that I find inappropriate, or inappropriate vis-à-vis my own world of dis-ease and dis-contentment. In this other person's—I wouldn't call it happiness, but her apparent happiness—in the lackadaisical quality of her trust, the seed of my envy is planted. Why does she have this ease and happiness? Why is it hers and not mine? And it doesn't make sense, but as I stand in the carpeted room, this is the question that's bugging me. I'm feeling it. Her abundance is creating a lack of abundance in me, a paucity to which I react, not with generosity or understanding, or even healthy competition, but with wormy invidiousness.

My response to her seeming confidence is like Claggart's response to the goodness and beauty of Billy Budd. It's a kind of envy in which the goodness and grace of this other person has to be canceled out.

"Take off your hat," she tells me.

"I'm not wearing a hat," I say.

"Figuratively, I mean. Relax."

So I try to seem relaxed. And that works for a while, and we talk for a while, about things, like the color of the car, and the profusion of bugs on the windshield, and all the time I'm talking to her I'm gauging her, waiting for her to trip, figuratively, so I can know whether she's had a party to play in Anne's disappearance. I already *think* she's had some part in it, but I want proof to make it all clear. Then she'll be bad and I'll be good and I'll feel better. But something about the room, or about her and her apparent honesty, is making me feel worse, and so, once she gives me the piece of paper with the telephone number, I fold it, put it in my back pocket, and then I tell her I have to go.

2

Later that day, through the curtains of my room, I watch the girl walk across the parking lot, but instead of getting into one of the cars, she walks past the cars, to the edge of the parking lot where it meets the circular drive. I leave my room and follow her, staying far enough behind her to avoid obviousness, but trailing her as she walks along the sidewalk. The sidewalk at this section of road is mostly a trail of hard-packed earth, through weeds sometimes and little puddles of water, and I note, at one point, her footprints.

At the intersection of the circular drive and one of the radial streets that feed the university there's a liquor store and she goes in. Rather than waiting outside, I also go in. Why not? I see her head looking into the refrigerated cabinets and I look at bottles of wine, all the time watching her. She's buying some kind of juice or fruit beverage and I'm thinking about her, and I'm also thinking about buying a reasonably priced California wine. I wait for her to pay for her fruit drink at the counter, and then, as she exits out the door, I decide to buy a disposable camera. I'm thinking it might come in handy, but when I pay for it, I'm about thirty-five cents short. The man behind the counter, with his combed gray hair, tells me to give him what I have, take the camera, and pay him later. The man insists I take it, and for some reason, looking at the man, and seeing beyond his bristly mustache and bad teeth to the generous smile forming on his cheeks, I do. I thank the man and tell him I don't need a bag. I hurry out of the liquor store because, like a good tracker, I don't want to lose my quarry.

But when I get outside, worried that she's gone off and that I'll have some catching up to do, I find her instead, standing right in front of me, wrestling with the plastic wrapper on her drink. I watch her for a long moment with a strange sense of pleasure and fulfillment. In a way I enjoy her struggle. I feel lifted by her momentary difficulty, and feeling garrulous, I speak to her. "Having a little trouble?" I say.

She looks up and smiles. "Protecting us from ourselves," she says, and when she finally gets the plastic removed from the bottle she throws the packaging into the trash and begins walking back to the motel.

That's where I would be going too, but because I don't want to seem to be following her, I don't move. I don't know if I should be walking with her or not, and so not knowing, I deal with my own packaging, and all the time I'm dealing with it I'm thinking about her, the way her hair fell, or was blown by the spring winds, across her face, and her collar pulled up against the wind, and her fingers, and her skin, a dark skin or softly tanned skin, and her mouth when she smiled. Standing there, I wish I would have remembered more of her, and other parts of her. I'm already forgetting so much, and I think, If only I had a better memory.

That's why I turn, follow her tracks, and catch up with her at the edge of a bulldozed field. It's empty at the moment, awaiting some future construction, and she's gone out there for some reason, to look around and breathe, and I find myself pulled out there as well, to her.

I say pulled because, although I'm holding my little camera, I couldn't really have said I had any reason to be following her. We're standing on the site of the future mini-mall, and nothing is said about the odd coincidence of our seeing each other twice in the same day.

"Are you taking pictures?" she says.

"Yes," I say, and lift the camera to prove it.

"Of?"

"Landscapes," I say. "Buildings mainly. And people, if they're around."

"Doesn't look very populated now," she says, indicating the pallets of cinder block.

"No," I say, and although I'm looking at her, I'm also seeing everything around her, the light and the air and the leveled dirt.

"Don't let me stop you," she says.

"As a matter of fact," I say, and I ask her if she'd be willing to stand in a picture. "To give scale," I say. And when she stands and strikes an appropriate pose, I adjust the composition. I ask her not to smile. She doesn't smile. "That's perfect," I say, and then I snap the picture.

"Take another," she says. "Sometimes the first one . . . In case I smiled."

"Okay," I say, and I take another.

"What about this?" she says, and she puts her foot on a stack of two-by-fours. I take the photo and when we stand together, afterward, she asks me why no smiling.

"So as not to distract from the landscape," I say.

"How would a smile distract from that?"

"You're right," I say. "It wouldn't."

And that's about all we say. We walk together to the motel, just walking along, the wind cool, the sun warm, just walking together until we get to the motel stairway, where we stop. I would like to keep walking, to continue on our common trajectory, and although she seems to enjoy being looked at, and I would like to keep looking, my room is in a different direction.

So we start to float apart, like two ice floes slowly flowing in different directions. I want to pull them (the ice floes) together so I say one more thing to her. I tell her she looks like Joni Mitchell.

"Maybe it's the beret," she says.

I shrug, and when she turns to go I say, "Who did you say you knew around here?"

"I didn't say," she says. "I'm with my friends."

And then she walks up to her room. And I imagine that happiness probably exists up there in that room, waiting. Not for me, but for her. "Good luck," I say, half aloud, either to her or the stairway she just walked up, and although I'm saying "Good luck" to her, I'm wishing that some of that luck was mine.

I can tell I need to sleep. I'm experiencing sleep deprivation, which is causing me to stand there long after she's walked away, not moving, staring at the concrete staircase. Later, in my own room, in my bed by the window, I think about her. I would like to go to sleep but I keep having these thoughts, and although they're *my* thoughts, they have a mind of their own.

3

In Melville's *Billy Budd*, the eponymous young sailor is called—in an expression from another time—a natural man. He's a man with grace and generosity of spirit. And Claggart, his nemesis in the story, can't stand the natural attraction people feel for Billy, including his own attraction. Holding on to the dwindling lie of his own superiority, he torments Billy and plots against him, and all because of his inability to live without some barrier between him and what he sees as a threat to what he believes he is. We don't know the whole history of Claggart so we don't know if maybe his obsession with destroying Billy Budd is a way to avoid looking at some lack of something in himself. But there he is.

And there I am, walking out my door to the motel parking lot, which is empty except for the dark Mercedes, nose to nose with the maroon station wagon. I walk across the parking lot, like walking across a frozen lake, walking to what may or may not be my old car, and when I get to the car, Linda is sitting behind the steering wheel rolling down the window.

"I see you're still fascinated by the car," she says.

"I didn't see you here," I say.

"No?" she says.

"No," I say. "Not really." Looking down from the scarf on her head to the handle of her door, I notice some pieces of broken glass beneath the left front tire of her car. I don't tell her about the glass, but because I want to think of myself as a good person, I offer her a ride in *my* car. "Do you need a ride?" I say.

"I'm fine," she says. And she notices that I'm looking at her door handle, not her, and she says, "Do *you* need a ride somewhere?"

"I have a car," I say, pointing to the Pulsar, which is parked by the empty swimming pool.

So she starts the car, and it sounds like the old maroon Tracer. I can see that when she drives away she'll drive over the glass, and you might think: How can I do that? How can I let her drive off with the glass beneath her tire?

How I do that is called interpretation. I'm trying, in my mind, to interpret my actions as the actions of a good person. But it's not that easy because, although I intend to tell her, and in fact am thinking of a graceful way to do it, at some level I want to deny her the happiness that ought to be mine, or had been mine, the happiness that I thought I wanted. As if, in the universe, there's only a limited amount of happiness and it's either hers or mine.

So when she puts the car into gear I'm waiting, still intending to say something about the glass on the ground, still intending to be good, but before I get an opportunity, she shifts the car back into park. She turns off the engine. "You know," she says, "I think I *will* take you up on your offer."

She gets out. And I'm a little nervous now, walking to my car, opening my passenger door and excusing my mess. She settles into the plastic seat and I get in behind the wheel and then I start the car.

"Thank you," she says. "It's pretty far away."

"I don't mind," I say. And as we drive off I can tell that she's looking at me, and that by looking at me she's giving me a signal to reciprocate.

But I don't.

She offers to pay me, but I say, "You just tell me where to go."

We drive along, past stoplights, moving with the flow of traffic until the town is behind us. The road begins to wind up into low hills. She's still looking at me, and I'm staring straight ahead, past the dashboard to the terrain outside.

"Have you ever gone *off* the road?" she says.

"You mean in an off-road vehicle or do you mean like . . . ?"

"What's your name?"

"Out of control?"

"What do people call you?" she says.

"Friends, you mean?"

"You must have a name."

"*Several* names. That *different* people call me."

"Does that mean you don't want to tell me your name?"

"What's your name?" I say.

"I already told you. I hate my name."

"Jack," I tell her.

"Like Kerouac."

"Linda," I say.

"Right. And your name is Jack."

I can feel her looking at the side of my face.

Although I'm not aware of any barrier or wall between us, there is something. And what it is, in a sense, is Anne, or my belief in Anne and my life with Anne, and because the person next to me is *not* Anne, I'm creating or constructing this particular wall or barrier or screen.

"Are you married, Jack?" she says.

"You mean because I don't wear a ring?" I say, lifting my left hand.

"I've never been married either. Officially," she says.

I look straight ahead and see the arc of the wiper traced on

93

the window, and the window itself. "Are the people you're with . . . I've noticed you're traveling with some people."

"You really like looking at the road," she says.

"I'm driving."

"But we're also talking."

"True," I say.

And she points to where I need to turn. "We're getting close," she says.

"What would I look at?" I say. "I mean I've noticed your friends, the people you're with . . ."

"Look at me, for instance."

And looking straight ahead I tell her, "I'm concentrating on the road."

"That's all right," she says. "Except maybe you've concentrated enough. It's not really all that complicated, is it?"

And I can feel a million things going on in my mind, and to avoid the confusion of all of them happening at once, I turn and look at her face.

"There," she says, pointing to a barn up ahead, off to the side. "You see that barn thing? That's the barn."

I slow down, turn right, and drive up a gravel driveway. I park on some level ground near a propane tank. I kill the engine. "We made it," I say.

She unties her scarf and shakes out her hair.

And it might not be clear from our words alone, but what was just happening was that I wasn't doing what she wanted me to do. I wasn't looking at her. I was seeming to be doing it, or seeming to be trying to do it, but I wasn't.

She wants a little attention and there's nothing wrong with that. She wants to break through the barrier between us, thinking that breaking through will make her happy. And maybe it would. But my happiness is different. My happiness—I wouldn't even use the word "happiness," my form of satisfaction—comes from keeping her from what she wants. She seems to have enough happiness as it is, and because I don't have enough or don't feel I have enough, I want to keep it from her. If I can't have it, no one will.

4

There's a red house nestled in the hill, and across the road there's a tumbledown chicken coop. An older man appears at the door of the house with a bright red stocking cap on his head, smiling and waving. He walks to her side of the car, and immediately they embrace. I watch the hug until, after a while, she introduces me, referring to me as a friend, and the old man walks over to me, looks into my eyes, takes my hand, and embraces me.

Together we walk to the house, the man leading the way. He and Linda are talking about work and people, and there's something strange, or at least I'm sensing something strange, and it isn't clear what it is until the man looks up, turns to me, and asks me who I am.

"I'm Linda's friend," I say.

"Linda?" he says. Then holding up his open palms he says, "Welcome."

His smile seems full of equanimity and acceptance, although it's possible it only seems that way. It's possible that only certain things, certain events or facts or people, get through the filter of his attention. Linda mentioned to me that her friend was losing touch, by which she meant he was losing his memory, and although he seems clear-headed, as we walk to the house I'm looking at the old guy, trying to discern any evidence of dementia or incoherence.

In the house there's a large, unlit fireplace, neat and orderly, and there's a desk by the window, neat and orderly and unused. The whole house is that way. The rugs are clean. At first we're all standing around, Linda and the old man exchanging different kinds of information, and at a slight pause Linda turns to me and says, "Would you like something?"

"You mean to drink?" I say.

"There's tea," the old man says.

"I could use a little liquid," I say, and it turns out the man has made some sun tea by leaving a glass jar of water and a tea bag sitting out on the back steps. "We have some in the refrigerator," he says, walking through an archway dividing the front part of the house from the kitchen, negotiating his way around the various pieces of furniture.

I join Linda on the large sofa, crossing my legs. She adjusts the material of her pants. I'm sitting on a crack between two cushions and she's sitting on a third cushion, and both the padding and the springs of the sofa are getting older, and the whole thing is not absolutely firm and so the sagging of the sofa draws the two of us closer.

There we are, sitting on the lumpy sofa, listening to the clinking of glass in the next room, and even for me, involved as I am with the past, the present moment is taking my attention. The old man calls out, "I'm putting in a little bit of sugar," and he returns with two glasses of tea with ice cubes. He's standing there, looking at the two of us, holding the tray, looking and standing, and she says to him, "Where would you like to sit?"

"I'm going to find your bathroom," I say, standing up as he sits down.

Mr. V.—that's what she's calling the man—explains the way but I assure him I can find it. And I do.

I'm in the bathroom and Linda is in the fireplace room, and

although we are separated by several walls, I imagine we're thinking about the same thing: each other. I'm wondering who she is, and if somehow she's responsible for the kidnapping of Anne, or the disappearance of Anne. And what about her friends? And bringing me up to this house in the forest? And this old man? What's that about? And I'm sure she's wondering who *I* am, this person who seems to be following her. And is he following her, or is she bringing him along? And if she's bringing him along, why? He seems like an honest person, the way he stands with his weight on one leg, his arm bent, but it doesn't mean he actually is.

When I come out of the bathroom, having been in a little world of my own thoughts, I'm aware that those thoughts have disconnected me from the world I'm standing in now. Like flies around my head, they're distracting me. There's always some thought, I think, and I try to push through the thoughts and come into the world. Which I do, briefly, looking at Linda, who's surrounded by pillows, sitting on the bedspread-covered sofa. I don't feel like sitting quite yet so I stand, with my weight on one leg, leaning against the fireplace.

The old man, Mr. V., is sitting in his comfortable chair, but he's sitting like a young man, legs spread, hands on thighs, looking intently and openly into Linda. I say "into" her because it's not just into her eyes. He's leaning toward her and you can feel the attention he's sending to her or washing over her. He's probably in his sixties or seventies or even his eighties and yet it's difficult to judge. He's thin, but his cheeks have the ruddiness of someone who's lived his life outside.

There's a bond between this man and Linda, and I don't know what *kind* of bond, but it's a bond. Linda occasionally turns to me, smiles, then turns back to the old man. I drink my tea. I'm still a married man, and I know I'm a married man, and I've made no overtures toward this Linda person, this person who means nothing to me, and may in fact be the villain in the story I'm right in the middle of.

I have, not only the memory of Anne, but the possibility of a future life with her. I believe in that future, and because Linda isn't Anne, I'm not really that interested in her. But because the man is interested in her, and she's obviously interested in the man, I'm starting to see the ease and fellowship happening in front of my face as a threat.

I try to say a few words or ask a few questions but I can't break the not-quite-palpable beam of emotional fellowship passing between them. It's not *my* emotional fellowship, and although I would want to be part of it, it seems to me a fellow-ship completely unattainable, or at least unenterable, and I feel now a definite wall separating me from what I want.

And maybe Linda can see this, because she stands and suddenly announces that she's giving me a tour. We walk outside and she begins showing me things, trees and mushrooms, and we walk to the old barn up the hill, a big insulated barn. The small door is unlocked and inside she shows me the cameras that were used when the man was actively photographing bats. The bats are all gone now and the barn and the studio are in disrepair. There are cages and lights and tripods and she explains how the bats would fly down, grab whatever food was offered, and the moment the food was snatched a trigger set off a strobe that flashed light and a photograph was taken.

She takes me into an office part of the barn and shows me photographs of bats, swooping down at millisecond intervals, their claws or talons reaching for morsels of food. Also on the wall, on a different part of the wall, are pictures of people, mainly women, including women in states of partial undress.

There's one particular photograph of a young woman and her

apparently nude body. It's very artistic. A close-up. She seems to be standing on a beach, but its focus is the woman's back, with part of her arm and part of her breast and the ripples of her stomach as she bends toward the sand. I can see in the tilt of her neck something about her personality revealed.

At first I don't say anything, just walk along the wall, photo after photo, black-and-white, and then, when I get to the end, I say, "These are very beautiful."

"Thank you."

"Is that you in some of them?"

"Some of them."

"That one?" I say, referring to the photo of the person bending.

"There's no beach around here," she says.

"It looks like you," I say. Then I realize I have no idea, or only a vague idea, what she looks like, like that. "It could be a sand dune," I suggest.

"Thank you, but I look nothing like that." She ushers me away from the photos and out of the room. "There's an album of photographs," she says, "back at the house."

"Who took them?"

"Mr. V."

"He likes you quite a lot," I say.

"I love him," she says. And then she adds, "How can you not?"

5

At a certain point the man suggests that he and I take a tour of the barn, and although I've already seen the barn, I agree. We put on our coats, go outside, and it isn't raining, but the earth is damp, and the trees that have fallen over are soft and moist and rotting. The trail we follow leads up a hill, past rock outcroppings, and eventually to a barn—a different barn than the other barn—and I help the man slide the large wooden door across the entrance to this barn, and we let ourselves in.

"How many barns do you have?" I ask him.

"Just the one," the man says.

It's filled with bales of sweet-smelling hay, and as we walk around the inside perimeter of this barn the man occasionally holds out his hand, and, to steady him, I take it. He sometimes rests his hand, or the fingers of his hand, on my shoulder, and although it's just a normal meaningless gesture, I feel it has a kind of meaning, a kind of generosity, and because I am thinking about generosity and looking at the piece of gauze bandage stuck to his face, I'm not sure if I'm hearing what the man is saying.

"War?" I say.

"There's always a war," the man says. "Or if there's not, then it's coming. Not out there"—and he points to his chest. "Here."

I'm going to ask him to elaborate but the man moves on. In his mind he's constantly moving on, not stopping for understanding or for the acknowledgment of understanding. He's moving, and I follow him.

The wooden planks are unevenly worn around the swirls of knots in the wood. I ask the man, "Do you still have bats?"

"I thought *you* were the expert on bats," he says, and he smiles.

And for some reason I smile back. "I thought *you* were."

"Well, there you go," he says, and laughs out loud, in a way that I find infectious. Not the laugh itself but the situation. I don't really know what, but something is amusing. And although I started out being jealous of his relationship with Linda, it's hard to be jealous of someone so genial. Although my usual modus would be to envy the man's seeming happiness, instead I can feel that seeming happiness making *me* seem to be happy.

I follow him through a narrow door into a structure with another door and we walk through that door and the old man starts climbing up the hay bales stacked in the corner. The barn is in disrepair. "Come on," he says. And because I don't feel at the moment like climbing up a stairway of old straw, I ask him, "What's up there?"

"The view," he says.

"Of what?"

"It won't hurt you," he says, "I promise," and he holds out his hand.

I would rather not have to depend on a withered old hand but I don't see a lot of options, so I reach out and the old man indeed pulls me up, into a small attic-like room. He closes the trapdoor and we find ourselves crouching in darkness.

As I wait for my eyes to adjust, I notice that my hands are raised, as if to defend myself. That's weird, I think, because there's nothing to be afraid of. I've been in pitch-black rooms before, but still, fear is not a logical thing. And it isn't until my eyes adjust and I can see the source of light that I know where I am and let my hands drop.

A camera obscura is a dark chamber with a hole on one side

and that's what we're in. Projected against the opposite wall of the room is an image—mainly sky, a few trees—and something about the color of the sky and the depth of the sky, despite the inverted view, makes it seem completely real. The image isn't large but it's large enough to hold, in its indistinct frame, the whole world. I'm looking at the image, watching the world it portrays—removed from it and watching it—like watching something die. It seems at that moment like a world of possibility.

"I don't get up here much anymore," the man says, and then he opens the hatch, and when we crawl out into the normal light, the possibility doesn't vanish.

We climb back down the hay and I don't mind the straw in my socks. I like it. I like everything. I feel energized, buoyed, and the feeling has something to do with the man, or the presence of the man, who is smiling, narrow-shouldered but erect, looking at me as if I am a source of pride. The watery whites of his eyes are cloudy, but the dark center, from behind which he seems to be looking, is bright.

When the man speaks, the words coming out of his mouth are reassuring, or have the intention of reassuring. For instance, "On the road." He says these words out loud, infusing them with nobility, declaring them as a state of being. "On the road."

"That's right," I say.

"You were on the road," he says, and he says it with a seriousness that stills me. He is looking at me.

"Yes," I say.

"I can see," he says. And it seems as if suddenly he's lucid. "Do you know what's happened to you?"

"You mean about my wife?" I say. And the man doesn't answer.

I think what he sees is some truth about me, not a secret inside of me, but what I am. And he can see that I don't know myself what that is, and so all he can do is stand there, with a bandage on his cheek, looking at me with his watery, compassionate eyes.

Once we're outside, I try to slide the barn door shut by myself, but it's stuck. I am trying to do a good deed by closing the door but I can't get it rolling on its rollers. Even with both hands, even leaning into it with all my weight, the gate doesn't move. At which point the old man holds the side of it, pulling it onto its tracks. He tells me to try again, and this time, on its rollers, the thing easily slides shut.

"Thanks," I say.

"You'd do the same," he says.

And then he starts walking, looking down at the path of his feet. When he gets to the house he turns around, having already forgotten who I am; but trusting whatever I am, he smiles and walks inside. I would like to follow. I like his house and I like him, and although I want to stay with him, I can't.

6

As human beings we have an idea of who or what we are, and we like to keep that idea intact. And although this desire for a sense of self isn't a sin, like a sin we can get excessive about it. Two hundred years ago Keats spoke about the ability to live without definite answers and borders, and because I'm a man who makes adjustments, at the moment I'm willing to do that. At the moment I'm with Linda, following her directions, driving with her, and I'm willing to know nothing but what's in front of me, or in this case next to me, in the car. And not only am I willing to simply see her, I'm also willing to send her something, something reassuring. I'm trying, in some quasi-physical way, to send her something good.

But how do you do that? How do you wish another person well? It's probably not so difficult, but with her I'm having a little trouble. And the trouble is Anne. I need to believe that Anne will remain in my life, but at the moment Anne's not here.

Linda and I are driving deeper into the woods, into steeper, more rugged country, and at a particular turnoff she tells me to pull over, and I pull off the main road onto a rutted dirt road and we drive up that road until we come to the end. We get out of the car, walk up through a trail in the grass, and arrive at a clearing at the top of a hill. There's a metal structure, with a platform at the top, a lookout above the trees, open to the elements.

"There's the view," she says. "Up there."

And then she walks down a slight incline to another part of the clearing. There's a pool, a reflecting pool made of stone, aban-doned now, covered with lichen and moss, built by human hands a long time ago. There's a shallow layer of water in the pool and she doesn't walk in the water at first. Instead she walks along the stones describing the pool's perimeter. The sun is shining enough so that she feels like taking off her shoes, which she does. She's dancing from stone to stone, and she knows I'm watching, and although she doesn't know who I am, it doesn't seem to matter.

And I'm thinking along the same lines. That who she is is partly transparent, or rather the outside of who she is is transparent. I see through the layer of linen pants and skin to something else, to a person. It's an image of her and it's *my* image of her, and as I watch the image of her I'm thinking about Anne.

When we were first getting to know each other, before we'd even had sex, Anne and I took a trip to the beach. It was summer and she was wading into the tidepools with her pants rolled up and a light shirt on and the waves on the rocks and I always suspected she got wet so that I would see her and want her, and if that was her plan it worked.

And you might think that I would be thinking of that time with joy and happiness, but I'm not. Those times, I'm begin-ning to think, are gone. With my feet in the present and my mind in the past, my emotional attachment to that memory is beginning to fade. And I would be willing to let it fade, except even if it's part of a past chapter in my life with Anne, there are other chapters coming, chapters filled with love and inti-macy. I'm thinking that what existed in my past was love and that you can't manufacture love or manufacture passion, and a person has to believe that those things—love and passion and life itself—will exist again, in the future.

I say I'm thinking, but it's not so much thinking as telling myself. I'm trying to influence my thoughts. And also my feelings, the thoughts of my body. Somewhere in my body I'm enjoying what's happening now. I'm enjoying the splashing of, and proximity to, this other person, and although I'm not *trying* to cancel the past or filter it out, I'm afraid that what is happening now will cause Anne to disappear.

To the extent that we make our own future, I want to make one I can hold on to. I need Anne, sure, but what exists right now is real. I am real and Linda is real, and real things have a certain attraction, and so I turn to Linda, and when she looks back at me I don't do anything. I don't try to change or correct or filter anything out. I let Linda be Linda. It just happens. And the fact of its happening is frightening because I'm not used to Linda. But I tell myself—looking at her—that what is happening is reality. Whether I'm making it or not, the sun is shining. Part of the rectangular pool is cast in light and part in shade and she has pulled up her pants and she's splashing in the water, laughing occasionally in the sunlight.

I'm perched on the rock ledge, sitting in the sun, and when she splashes me I enjoy it. She's holding her shoes in her fingers, her socks tucked inside, and you'd have to call it dancing what she does. The sun drops down farther into the trees and the sunlight disappears and by the time she steps out of the water of the pool she's, not wet, but damp, and she's shivering. I loan her my jacket and without guilt or memory or sadness getting in the way, we sit. I hold her in my arms, feeling the coldness of her skin and the warmth beneath that skin.

When Anne lived above the flower store on Sixth Avenue it happened like this many times. I came in the door and there she was, demure and polite but obviously excited, her etiquette not intending to mask her excitement. And without much talk we removed our clothes and then she jumped onto me. Her legs spread around my hips and I was lifting her and holding her so that her chest was level with my nose and mouth, and then lowering her down, and without any help from any hands we came together like that, sometimes her arms getting tired from holding on and sometimes my legs getting tired supporting her, and when this preliminary congress was over, I carried her to the bed and we fell finally, relaxed, into each other's arms. And then showering, and in the shower if the mood was right, we would repeat ourselves.

And whatever love existed then, that was one thing, and each moment a new love takes its place. And I can see this person next to me, and I can see the possibility of love, and the only reason not to love is Anne, because I still love *her*. I can feel the regret and loss, and sitting next to me is something else, something that isn't regret or loss. But there's nothing I can do because in my heart, love and loss and regret are all combined, and I have my need, and my need is to find the thing that's lost.

That's when Linda stands up. She stands up, out of my arms, and starts tiptoeing away through the water. It seems to me she wants to be on her own, so I stand up. I walk to the tower at the top of the hill. I look up the rungs of the metal ladder and then begin climbing it, rung by rung, straight up, concentrating on the individual rungs as I come to them. And when I get to the top, to the perforated metal platform, I look down and she's still there, walking through the pool. I look out and can see over the rolling hills, and although the sky is filled with clouds I can see the horizon in 360 degrees. The expression "takes your breath away" would be appropriate here because my heart or lungs seem to fill with so much air that it's difficult to breathe. I'm looking off in all the various directions, and although I'm looking at the view, I'm thinking about Anne.

Remember the bathtub? That claw-foot bathtub? That was probably your favorite place to be. I remember when we were first going out, still getting to know each other. I was in bed, not sleeping, just lazing around, and you got up. I felt you get up, crawl over me, and I remember the water running and you were gone. And you stayed gone. And I began to wonder what happened to you. And when you continued to stay gone I got up and followed the silence, because by then the water had stopped flowing and it was absolutely quiet. And I didn't knock, I just very slowly opened the door to the bathroom. A candle was burning on a little white table you had—this was your apartment on Ninth Street—and the candle was the only light. You were in the tub, naked of course, and what I remember was your beauty. We'd made love before so I'd seen you naked, but this was a different kind of nakedness. You saw me, you looked at me, but nothing changed because of me. You were there, in the tub, and you let me look at you, just as you were letting the sink and the toilet and the candle look at you. You were existing, without façade or artifice. Just being. And I stood there for some time, a long time, seeing your body in the tub, with the water of the tub still and smooth, your face damp, your eyes open, desireless, and you were looking at me. It was the most relaxed you'd ever been with me, the most available you'd ever been. That was the moment you let the world—and I was part of that world—see you. And it could have been my moment too, but it wasn't. Even though you were sharing it with me, and were willing to share it with me, I didn't feel it was mine. It was something I seemed incapable of understanding, or deserving, and because it was your moment, I envied you for having it. Later, I washed your back and then other parts of your body and we talked and laughed and I got wet and days went by, but that moment, that long moment when you lay stretched out under the clear water, because of that one time seeing you, pure and effortless and still, I never saw you again in quite the same way. I never saw you again as beautiful because I never wanted you to be as beautiful as in that moment. In my mind I was always comparing myself with who you were when you were perfect. You know what they say. "Things happen," and "Life goes on," and now I'm here, standing under the sky, thinking of you—somewhere—under the same sky, and when I imagine you, the person I see is the person you were, the person submerged in the water, looking back at me, your eyes filled with what I wanted. But at the time I didn't realize how much I wanted it.

7

Linda and I drive back to the motel. As we stand at the back stairway, as she's about to say goodbye and head up the stairs that lead to the second floor, that's when her friends come out. I meet the other girl and the guy. They've been worried, but now they're smiling and friendly, glad to meet this new fellow, named Jack, who she introduces.

They all seem nice enough but I'm not saying hello. And the reason I'm not is that I'm wondering who they really are and what they know about Anne. I'm not saying, "Nice to meet you," because I'm asking them questions. I've looked at the car, with its California license plate, but I still haven't convinced myself it isn't my car.

I ask them about the gas station in New Jersey. They tell me they've never been there. I ask them why they're driving separate cars, and the man—the other woman is quiet—tells me, in a British accent, that they're taking a car to his mother, that it's his mother's car and they're driving it for her.

Standing there in the middle of the stairway, I'm vaguely aware that I'm speaking too loudly, with too much excitement, but I can't help it. I'm seeing them across some kind of gap, and because it's *my* gap, they don't quite understand. They seem to be honest, friendly, good-looking people telling me about their trip, and the more they talk, the more I realize they're actually telling me the truth.

And thank god for envy, because without it I could easily

let their honesty open my eyes. I could very easily believe that the car is not my car, and convince myself of that. It's amazing how little attention I'd actually given my car when it *was* mine. It was just a car. Nothing I took the time to notice really, so that now, faced with my lack of awareness, I'm wishing I'd lived a little differently. If I had I might know. And because I don't know, I feel lost. I have no idea what I'm doing, only that I have to keep doing it. I started with a belief that used to be mine, and now that belief is a habit, so I keep it alive.

In my, not heart or mind, but in my sadness and my desperation, and my desire to keep my life intact, I can't believe them. And at the same time I can't *not* believe them. I'm caught in the gap of envy, between what I want to be happening and what actually is. And what I want is surety. No negative capability for me. I want what they have. I envy them their ability to move forward with ease and confidence. Although they're not all Americans, they have the confidence and complacence of Americans, the attitude of ownership that makes them seem American. And since I'm also American, I want the same set of sureties. Although I despise the attitude, I want the kind of confidence which might protect me from the desire for things to be different. And I don't feel I have it.

They're talking to me and saying things to me and I'm making appropriate responses. There's still the gap between where I am (with the well-intentioned people) and where I want to be (with my belief that they're the cause of my pain), but after a while, maintaining that gap is just too difficult. Without knowing it and without intending it, I step out of the limbo of that gap, break through the membrane between what I want to believe and what is there. These people are there and I see what they are, and however briefly, I see that they're not the lovers of

Anne or the abductors of Anne. I see, through my own needs and desires, to them.

"Are you staying in Lexington?" I say, and the man, whose name is Geoff, says that they're driving on. To Colorado. "Where in Colorado?" I ask, and he tells me they have some friends outside of Boulder. "Really?" I say. "That's where I'm going."

"Maybe we'll see you," he says, and they all nod, and I tell them sure, maybe so.

And then I let them go. In my mind I let go of the idea that the maroon car is my car, and that these people are somehow my enemies. There's a difference between wanting what they have and wanting them not to have it, and I say good night.

I go back to my room. I lie on my bed, my feet crossed, looking up at the plaster of the ceiling. I stare at the cracks in the plaster, seeing the branching lines become like hieroglyphs, and as my eyes defocus, the picture formed by the lines becomes more and more abstract, and after a while the lines are gone and even the ceiling is gone, and I see, in my mind, the gas station in New Jersey.

I see Anne, pulling up in Chaucer, bending forward, looking at me from the driver's seat. I'm coming out of the convenience store. She's sitting in the car, her hands on the steering wheel, and then suddenly there's a blur in my peripheral vision. A dark car, the sound of brakes, and the car driving by. I remember cursing the driver for coming so close, for possibly hitting my car. I remember checking the side of the car, thinking they might have scraped it as they passed. I remember Anne's face, looking up at me through the window.

In the morning, as is my habit, I part the curtains to check on the two parked cars in the parking lot. Both the cars are gone.

I make coffee at a miniature coffeemaker in the room, and

113

then I get dressed. I set my room key on the television, go to my own little car, and as I leave the circular road and drive to the highway entrance I run into a traffic jam. I get out, walk past the idling cars in the street, and there, at the front of the line of cars, is a procession, a procession of children dressed in sparkling costumes, some as animals, some as gods or goddesses. A portable music device is playing dance music, and the children have learned the steps and they're dancing to the music. Parents are walking alongside, watching, and more than just parents, the whole community is participating in the event. Even I, standing by a stall with a woman selling Mexican food, am part of it. I buy a taco from the woman, and when the dance is over I get back in my car. Everyone else is driving away, going where they have to be going, and so that's what I do.

IV

Luxuria

1

Human beings have a barrier, a membrane that separates our everyday life from our sexual life. I call it the sexual membrane. It's a protective device, enabling us to function in a day-to-day way during the day, but also, by lifting it up or pulling it aside, a sexual, passionate part of ourselves is also available. Anne had such a thin membrane it was sometimes hard to tell what side she was on. Not that she was always thinking about sex, or engaging in sexual activity, but that to go from the everyday side to the sexual side took very little effort. Which is the beauty of the membrane: this permeability. It's possible to go back and forth as many times as you want. And although it's designed to allow for easy crossing, from one side to the other, sometimes, when you're on one side of the membrane, you tend to forget that the other side exists.

And it's not just sexual.

Driving through the river valleys and rolling hills of the mid-section of America, through St. Louis and Kansas City and Topeka, I rarely stopped to eat. I was stopping for gas because the car needed gas, but food and eating had become ideas only, and I was losing interest in them. Driving along with my arm out the window I was unworried about sunburn, uninterested in the scenery or the historical markers. I was just driving, determined to keep Anne uppermost in my thoughts. And she was. My mind flitted from thought to thought and she was there all right, but the thoughts I had did not engender the feeling I wanted.

My thoughts were connected to loss and sadness and I was looking for more positive and motivating emotions. Loss and sadness had their place, but their tendency was to pull me into myself, and I wanted to pull myself out, into the world. And the problem, I thought, was desire. If I would have a little more desire then my thoughts—and by virtue of my thoughts, my life—would automatically focus on the world and enter the world and pull me away from my suffering.

Elaborate systems of enlightenment are built around the idea of desirelessness, but with me it seemed to bring, instead of enlightenment, only confusion and directionlessness. And I didn't like that. For me, feeling desire was synonymous with feeling alive, which is why I was looking out across the vast passing country for a place to pull off the road.

The color of this particular part of the earth was chalky and red. Scattered plants were turning green on the skin of the landscape, and my eyes were scanning the landscape, looking for a certain kind of spot, not sure what the spot would look like, but certain I'd know it when I saw it.

And when I did see it, I pulled off the highway. I was about a half hour outside of Salina, Kansas, and I parked the car in a small gravel area at the side of a county road. I walked through some weeds and crossed over a sagging barbed-wire fence into a sandy opening in the trees near a streambed, with rocks and roots and water flowing past. I settled myself in the sand of this area, and under the sun, fortressed by rocks and brush, that's where I pulled down my pants and began to try to masturbate. I say *try* because I wasn't feeling especially sexy or sexual or turned-on. I just wanted to feel what those things felt like.

Something in me was definitely willing, at least to try, to bring into my mind some fantasy, or a series of fantasies, and they came and went, but something else in me was either not willing or just not interested. I was distracted by something, or worried about something, and although I tried, I was disconnected from a part of myself, from Anne and the memory of Anne. I was disconnected from my body, and the excitement that resided in my body. But as I say, I tried to make it happen, to make desire happen, and I got to a certain point and I decided . . . I didn't decide. I changed my mind. The moment wasn't right, or the surroundings weren't right. I walked back to the car, got in, drove back to the main road, and continued on my westward trail.

Desirelessness can be a good thing, no doubt about it, but for me desirelessness was not the cessation of desire, it was the loneliness of no desire. Losing Anne was, in my imagination, the same as losing everything. And although I still believed I would find Anne, and still desired to find her, the membrane between me and my desire, I could feel, was thickening. I wanted to puncture the membrane or open the membrane, and to do that, even in my mind, I had to make an effort. And this effort involved focusing on Anne. Which was easy enough, except my thoughts alone weren't getting me through the membrane. The memories came but not the breaking through.

I remembered the time I bought Anne a negligee. She didn't want a negligee but she put it on and stood as she supposed I wanted her to stand, and it wasn't the sexiness of the garment that aroused me; it was her willingness to wear it. Her willingness was what I remembered, and it's what I was thinking about when, after driving along without music or human interaction, I stopped somewhere on the plains of Kansas and got some gas. A short distance down the road leading back to the interstate, at the edge of the gas station, two people, a man and a woman, were sitting with a few bags. I slowed down as I approached, pulling to a stop in front of them.

2

They said they were coming from a festival, and from the way they were dressed—he with the long hair, she with a feather in her braided hair—you might have guessed the Woodstock festival, or a Woodstock reunion. They were polite and appreciative, and as they put their canvas bags in the back seat they said they were going to Boulder, Colorado, which was where I was going.

The man, whose name was Fletcher, did most of the talking. The girl, whose name, appropriately, was Feather, sat in the middle of the back seat. She had lips like the lips of Brigitte Bardot, and I could see, in the rearview mirror, that her light brown hair was cut very short in front, so that it stood up, as in photos I'd seen of Chief Joseph, the last great chieftain of the Nez Perce Indians. Although Feather didn't talk much, her wide eyes were full of enthusiasm. Life for her was all about learning and growing, and since I'd been overlooking those aspects of life, I found her innocence and honesty attractive. Fletcher was also attractive and honest, and I was glad to have them in the car.

During the getting-to-know-you stage I asked them questions about themselves and it didn't take much to get them talking about their theory of love, which was really a theory of desire, according to which, love was just an echo of desire. "There's only desire," Fletcher said, and that's what they were after, a state of continual desire in which love would flourish. It wasn't pleasure exactly, but like pleasure, it existed for itself. To have desire—and specifically desire untethered to an object—"You have to get through all the other stuff, society's stuff." You had to get past the craving for outcome.

Although I challenged them occasionally, mostly I was interested in how they actually practiced what they were preaching. Because I was thinking about Anne, the idea of desire unconnected to an object made no sense to me, at least at the moment. But I was willing to listen. And they were willing to explain to me, and even show me, what they meant. At one point Feather actually pulled down her drawstring pants, enough to show me the tattoo of two arrows intertwining on her abdomen.

The back seat was small, especially with their luggage, but at some point Fletcher climbed in the back with Feather and I could see in the rearview mirror that they seemed to be in love. They would have called it something else, but whatever it was, they stayed there in the back seat, nestled in their canvas packs. I would occasionally look back at them and occasionally my eyes met Feather's, and although she didn't look like Anne, her eyes reminded me of Anne. They seemed to be saying, "Remember this? Remember desire, existing without cause or reason?" They seemed to be trying to show me how thin the veil was between the desire side and the other side, not talking, but in a way urging me to break through to that side, giving me a pretty clear invitation to cross the boundary to what I wanted to imagine, and the only problem was, I was driving the car. Instead of watching them I turned my attention to the fence posts that were racing past the highway.

We drove across the flat expanse of prairie, watching the snow-covered peaks of the Rocky Mountains coming into view. As we drove through Denver and up to the town of Boulder, I told them a version of my story, and they seemed optimistic about the probability of finding my wife. If desire, physical desire, was in me, and if I could access it, they practically guaranteed I would do what needed to be done. Both of them, they said, could see a little bit into the future. Fletcher said, "You can tap into the other world," and they both nodded as if they were acquainted with that other world.

When we pulled into Boulder I found a pay phone and called the number Linda had written on the piece of paper. The British fellow answered, and he gave me directions to a house in the foothills outside of Boulder. My two companions didn't seem to have a place to stay so I invited them to come with me. They accepted the invitation and we drove up several roads to a mailbox in front of a driveway. A man with dreadlocks pointed out where we could pitch a tent—they had a tent—and when we found a nice flat spot on the pine needles, that's what we did.

Other people were camping on the property around this house but they were barely visible through the trees. We laid our sleeping bags in the tent, which was probably a two-person tent, but they didn't mind and I didn't either. Not only did I have my sleeping bag, now I had—it wasn't a teepee but I thought of it as a teepee—the sense of being an Indian. Light came in from the top of the tent, and also from the walls, which were made of thin, green nylon. Since there was going to be a gathering that evening Feather and Fletcher decided to walk up to the center of where that gathering would be. I lay back on my unfurled sleeping bag, watching the sky pass by over my head and listening to the generalized hum of voices preparing for the party.

It wasn't the first time we met, but close to the first time. I had gone to Morgan's house. She lived in the back of her store, and the store was closed but as usual there were some people there, men and women, and one of the women was you. A bottle of bourbon was being passed around and there were bottles of beer. Everyone was guzzling and I remembered sitting around a fire. There couldn't have been a fire, not in the middle of a downtown store, but there was some focal point and, at least gesturally, people were warming their hands around whatever it was. And then the people began to leave. After a while it was just two couples, Morgan and her friend, plus you and your new friend—which was me—and we moved to the bedroom, which was just a bed against the wall in the back of the store. One thing led to something else and kissing was involved. We were showing each other, first our legs and then our buttocks, and you were eager to show your butt. You wanted to have a butt contest where we'd all show our butts. In a contest of butts you were sure you could win. Morgan's friend was getting excited and I was getting moderately excited, and then the something else led to hands on bodies and pressure on bodies, and although mostly our clothes stayed on, desire was established. And enough of it so that the pull of desire brought us together, brought me across that gulf or membrane, and together the chain of events led us to live with each other, to fall in love and live whatever that love, and the pleasure of that love, would be.

3

I found Linda and her two friends, Geoff and Lisa, sitting on a picnic bench in front of a large canvas yurt. Linda stood up when she saw me approaching and met me on the dirt road leading to the yurt. I could tell that something was going on, that a familial powwow was in progress, and that this probably wasn't a very good time to talk.

But I wanted to talk. "I was looking for you," I said.

"I'm glad you made it," she said.

"This is nice," I said, turning and looking generally around the area.

We stood there, and I have to say it was slightly awkward. She looked at me and she seemed glad to see me, but the conversation didn't seem to go anywhere.

"How was the drive?" I said.

"It was fine," she said.

She smiled at me in an apologetic way, and I could tell she felt impelled to get back to her friends, so I told her I'd see her later, at the party.

"Definitely," she said, and we both turned and walked away.

By the time I got back to the house the celebration had already started. People on the porch were playing guitars and singing, and there was a punch bowl and people were drinking and dancing, swaying and twirling to the music. I drank from the bowl and I was introduced—or introduced myself—to a number of people, all from the same social tribe, all wearing loose-fitting garments and carefully uncared-for hair. Smiling, and not just outwardly, these friends—the community of people that lived in and around the tents and the house—were living a kind of cliché, but as I stood with them, in the middle of it, they didn't seem at all false or pretentious.

Someone had built a sweat lodge just down a trail from the house, and people would leave the area around the house and then return later, hair wet and faces flushed. I joined a group— one man had a flashlight—walking down to this sweat lodge and what it was was a stick structure like an igloo, covered in plastic, with a fire outside. Red-hot rocks were brought from the fire into the tent and doused with water. About six or eight people were sitting cross-legged in the sweat lodge, all naked and sweating, and when I saw Feather standing at the entrance, steam rising off her body, her hair braided like the famous Indian chief she was emulating, I didn't fall in love because I was still thinking about Anne. But I saw her beauty. Even from a sidelong view her nakedness revealed a beauty of purity, or a purity of beauty, and yes, Anne had purity, and she also had a sense of humor, but while Anne was uppermost in my mind, I was somewhere else, not in the upper regions, but somewhere below that, in my belly, which was feeling unusually taut as I took off my shirt and my shoes. When I was completely undressed and about to step into the tent, expecting to see Feather either fully or partially dressed, there she was, still naked, still standing outside the igloo entrance, still dripping from the steam. She was standing in front of me with her cowlick hair, and I was just bringing my eyes down from her hair to her face when she kissed me. She sort of jumped up quickly, and kissed me on the lips, and then she walked away.

What that kiss had meant was something I tried to figure out, turning it around in my mind. And when I took my turn in the steam tent, sat in the circle, watching the rocks glowing in the center of the circle, and when I thought of the person who'd kissed me, when I pictured her, it was Anne. As the heat radiated off the rocks, the images that came into my mind were images of Anne. One image especially, of her, innocently standing on the rocks at a tide pool, letting herself get splashed by a wave, and her thin yellow shirt getting wet and transparent, and then her turning to me.

After the sweat lodge I went back to the main celebration, stood with my cup of punch, a little away from the main group physically, yet feeling oddly connected to the general hubbub.

And not just to the people.

I wandered down a pine-needle path away from the house, wandering along until I came to a tree. Slowly, I approached the tree, stood close enough to smell the tree, and listen, and look at the tree, not as a thing but as another life. I began to feel a tenderness for the tree. The old gnarled bark seemed beautiful to me, expanding and contracting in front of me, and the life of the tree (the force that through the green fuse moved) seemed visible to me, and when I touched the tree, put my hand against the hard bark, I could feel the yearning and sadness of the tree.

Or my own yearning and sadness.

Whatever it was it seemed to be pure. I wanted to talk to the tree. I knew that talking to a tree was not a normal thing to do, and yet I felt like reassuring the tree, comforting the tree as it stood before me. Longing is the desire for something unattainable, and while I couldn't afford to long for Anne, because that implied unattainability, I could—and did—feel longing for the tree.

I stayed there awhile and then I walked back to the tent. Feather and Fletcher were inside the tent, sitting cross-legged on the sleeping bags, their hands on each other's thighs. They invited me in and Fletcher told me about the LSD in the punch. Which didn't matter to me. I sat down, also cross-legged, creating a triangle inside the tent, and we didn't speak. The party voices were audible in the distance.

Fletcher turned toward Feather and looked at her. And then he looked at me. I looked at him and she looked at me, and we were all looking at each other in a way that made it unclear who was looking at who, or whom. Either way, there was a lot of looking going on. And at some point Fletcher slid across the sleeping bags, and with his fingertips, he began touching the base of my neck, pressing against my spine and spiraling his fingers down the bones of my back.

In the car, when they'd talked about sexuality, they'd talked about a desire that transcended mental and emotional and even physical accoutrements. They'd talked about the possibility of reaching that place of untainted desire, and now it seemed they were practicing it.

My encounter with the tree—the smell of the pine sap was still sticking to my fingers—had left me calm and surprisingly peaceful. As Fletcher continued kneading my back I was facing Feather, who was sitting very still, looking at me, letting me look at her, and something in her look, or the permission in her look, let me change her, or try to change her, into something else. And it wasn't that Feather became Anne, or that the bones in her wrist and the hairs on her arm became Anne's bones and Anne's hairs, but because I wanted Anne, even though she was Feather, I was feeling the excitement of being with Anne.

That's when Fletcher left the tent. He nodded to me as if he was giving me something, giving me an experience or a wish, or giving me Feather. He seemed aware of what was happening. He said, "If that's what you want," and what he was doing by saying "If that's what you want" was stepping aside. I don't imagine it was easy for him, but he was trying, I think bravely, to live the principles he advocated. Then he left the tent.

When he was gone Feather turned so that she was facing me directly. When she'd adjusted her position so that she was sitting close enough to reach out, she did. Our eyes were fixed on each other and she reached out, took my hand, and placed it on her heart. It wasn't exactly her heart because it was higher than her actual heart and more toward the edge of her chest, so that beneath the material of her shirt—between my hand and her heart—I could feel the outline of her breast. She was saying, "Feel my heart," and although that was something Anne would never say, I wanted to feel the heart, and feel the person, or radiance even, emanating from that heart.

Because in my mind it was partially Anne's heart, it was also Anne's breast, and I felt something stirring. I felt the stirring of desire, but every time I tried—or thought about—acting on this desire, I thought of Anne, and then the desire faded. And Feather seemed to understand this. It didn't seem to be a problem for her. I was all part of weeding out impurities. She was willing to accept whatever my so-called impurities might be, without judgment. And because human experience is full of complexity it's possible to have simultaneously conflicting impulses.

Which I did.

I say conflicting because certain of these impulses—about what I should do, or ought to do (or about Anne)—were holding me back, separating me from where part of me wanted to go. And the reason I didn't follow these impulses and break through any membrane was that I wasn't convinced I wanted to go there. I was dreaming of passing through to the other side, but at the same time I wanted to stay on the side I was already on. I was still with Anne or the memory of Anne. I knew that memories get superseded by desire, and because I was worried about losing Anne, I held on to her memory, in my mind. And I wouldn't say that I was fighting a battle between memory and desire, because memory also was desire.

All the time I was thinking this my hand was shivering.

"It's just a breast," she said.

"I'm fine," I said.

And something about my saying that brought my attention back to my hand, feeling the heat from her body, the softness of the flesh, and the structural framework of the body beneath that flesh.

But I didn't cross to the other side. She's there, I thought, on one side and I'm on the other side. And yes, I could have gone over and joined her except for the membrane. The thing about the sexual membrane is, once you're on one side, the other side seems very far away.

We sat like that for what seemed like a long time, and although I was looking into her eyes and she was looking into mine, what our eyes were saying were different things. I didn't know about my eyes, but her eyes were saying, "You almost made it. Almost, but not quite."

4

Feather, still looking into my eyes, raised a finger and tapped me on my chest, gently pressing her finger into my breastbone. I felt the sensation passing through my skin and through my breastbone, and I didn't think I'd asked any question but, as if answering a question, she took my hand and led me along a path in the pine trees to a Volkswagen van parked on a dirt road in the middle of a clearing. Fletcher was already in the van, the door open, eating rice from a bowl, using chopsticks. The whole back of the van was a platform with a foam pad and sheets, and when Feather and Fletcher began taking off their clothes, I assumed that they would want to be together when whatever was going to happen started happening. Which was fine with me. And when it did start to happen—first some light touching of feet, then rubbing of feet and ankles and lower legs—I was ready to go. As I started to squeeze past Feather she took my hand and placed it on Fletcher's foot. She grabbed his other foot herself and together we began rubbing. I imitated her massaging style, using my fingers and the knuckles of my fingers to dig as deeply as I could into the emotion-filled muscles and fascia of the ball of his foot. I could hear raindrops hitting the roof of the van when Fletcher sat up, took me by my shoulders, and positioned me so that I found myself straddling Feather, who was lying on her stomach. My hands were kneading her large gluteus muscle, and Fletcher was behind me, rubbing my back through my shirt. I still had my clothes on, unlike Feather, who turned over, so that I was now massaging her neck and her legs and everything between.

The whole interweaving dance had a mind of its own, and it continued until, at a certain point, Fletcher was massaging my back, and Feather was massaging Fletcher's back, and the only person not massaging was me, flat on my stomach, face tilted to one side, eyes closed, feeling the skin of my neck and back and buttocks exposed to the air. I could feel my belt being unbuckled and I knew that hands were touching me but I couldn't tell whose hands they were. And when I heard the metal doors of the van swing open I couldn't tell who left or who came until I heard Fletcher's voice asking me to turn over. And when I did I could see that Feather was gone. I could see that I was aroused, and I could feel it, but I was too relaxed or too lost in experience to do anything but notice.

One aspect of the sexual membrane is that once you're on the sexual side, you don't really care what happens next. In a sense I'd gone to a movie, and I was watching the movie, and at some point—I didn't know when—the movie became a different movie, and by the end of the movie I was enjoying whatever movie I was watching, and had forgotten a switch had occurred.

And as Fletcher continued massaging, the distinction between sexual organ and other organs—skin, say, or brain—disappeared, and in the middle of that disappearance I experienced something. I wouldn't call it cataclysmic, because it was effortless and sudden, and while I and my body were experiencing all the physiological things that happened in the aftermath of that, Fletcher unrolled some toilet paper. Even wiping my stomach was a kind of massage, and it wasn't absolutely clear if clean-shaven Fletcher, his hair tied out of his face, was being sexual. There was no sign of that. It was only clear that he was attempting to be kind, and for me, at the receiving end, there wasn't any difference between attempting to be kind and being kind itself.

Of course when it was all over I went back to the other side of the membrane, the nonsexual side. Fletcher became no longer a pair of practiced hands dancing the dance of pleasure; now he was a stringy-haired hippie manqué, and while I still liked him, as a human being, I didn't want to be with him. So I decided to take a walk.

There was a trail that led up from the van into the hills and I walked on that trail up the hill until I came to a wooden ladder over what might have been an electric fence. I stepped over that, walked out into a field, and in the middle of this field I came to the proverbial two roads diverging. Actually they were two *trails* diverging, an unused fire road and a smaller trail worn into the hillside grass.

Normally it wouldn't have been a question. I would have just picked a trail and kept walking. But I'd been thinking about desire and the twin poles that comprised desire: want and need. There was moment-to-moment craving on the one hand, and on the other, something that led to long-term satisfaction and fulfillment. Like everyone else, I believed I wanted satisfaction and fulfillment, so I stood at this junction, looking at the two roads, one less traveled than the other, and I knew it wasn't just the two roads, it was the *meaning* of the two roads. I somehow imagined that my choice would determine, not only where I went, but by virtue of that choice, what my world would be. It wasn't that one road was Anne and one road was Feather; both roads were going in the same direction. It was merely a question of knowing what it was I needed, and based on that, where I needed to go.

When Blake said that the road of excess leads to the palace of wisdom, he didn't say how long the road would be, or which road it was, and so I stood, not transfixed, but not moving forward, looking at these two brown roads.

I'd read in a book one time that a way to break through a barrier is to talk to yourself, in a mirror, on LSD. I had no mirror, but I stood in this meadow, a green grassy meadow. Clouds were obscuring the moon but there was light enough to see, and there was one big tree sitting in the middle of this meadow and I went up to this tree and started talking. Not talking. I knew the tree couldn't talk, but I tried to imagine, if it did, how would the tree communicate? I tried to talk with the tree. I stood in front of the tree, sending signals, sending vibrations, trying to receive something, or hear something, to have the tree, not tell me what to do, but show me, so that I might know. And because it was spring some seeds were falling, and one seed came down like a whirligig and landed on my head. I brushed it off. That wasn't what I wanted. I was trying to communicate. I was trying to communicate with this tree.

Although the tree was probably sending me loads of signals or vibrations, nothing was getting through. There was a skin between the tree and me, a membrane separating us, and my strategy was to tear at the fabric of the membrane. I knew the membrane was a mental construct, and that all I had to do was step through that mental construct. I knew my decision about the two trails was not about the trails, but about how I walked on whatever trail I took.

And maybe I would have acted on this knowledge, except I was distracted by the rain that was falling. Also by the thunder and the lightning strikes that were moving their way across the eastern horizon. I didn't think about the danger of standing on a hillside in an electrical storm. I thought about the lightning, and the different kinds of thunder. Chief Joseph was named after a kind of thunder, and I thought about cracking thunder and brittle thunder and howling thunder and vibrating thunder—and also the rolling thunder that I imagined had been rolling for a very long time across the great midwestern plain to get to me. By counting the seconds between the flash and the thunder, and dividing that by some number, I might have estimated the lightning's distance. But instead, I stood there, a light rain falling against my face, waiting for the next burst of light, and then waiting for the sound of the light. I stayed on the slope as the rain stopped and the thunder moved away. I waited to see, when the clouds parted, if I could see any sign of the waning moon.

I didn't see any moon because the clouds never completely parted, but as I was waiting, that's when I remembered the gas station in New Jersey. I remembered the car, the dark Mercedes turning at the last moment, but not before hitting my car, my maroon car. Anne had said, "Get something to drink," and I was coming out of the convenience store. She'd pulled up to the door and I'd stepped off the curb. I was opening the car door, turning my body to sit down into the car, when I saw the flash of darkness, and then I felt the collision. Not a big collision, but I felt it. I got out, looked at Anne, who was looking straight ahead, arms on the wheel, in shock. The other car was still moving, and as it pulled out of the gas station onto the Palisades Parkway I ran after it and watched it merging into the larger road.

When I got back to the car Anne was shaking. She was nervously talking and I didn't notice the tears in her eyes because I was thinking about the damage and the people who caused the damage. I wanted to see what they'd done to my car. I wanted to see the dent they'd put in the side by the fender. The dark paint of the car had scraped away and replaced the old maroon color, and the wheel well was bent slightly. But that was about it. And I was reassured that that was it. I was alive at least, and Anne was alive.

5

The next morning I went to the now-deserted house and sat on an overstuffed chair on the porch. The air was full of the sounds of animals and birds and trees swaying. Pine resin was warming in the sun. I didn't find any coffee to make so I drank water. I drove into town and spent the morning driving around, looking for station wagons. I was fairly methodical in my walking up and down the various streets, undaunted by my lack of success. The Mercury Tracer wasn't a popular car so not that many were made, and there weren't that many—none maroon—on the streets of Boulder.

Sometime in the late afternoon I wandered into the pedestrian mall. On a side street off the mall I discovered, in a large community building, a poetry class in progress. I was tired so I sat in a chair in the back of the room, listening to people talking about Beatniks, and about various poets. A man, with a beard like Allen Ginsberg's, standing beneath an uplifted basketball backboard, began talking about William Carlos Williams.

Apparently there's a poem by William Carlos Williams in which a man stops his car, lets his kids off at school, then drives to where the road ends, and from there walks down to the edge of the river. Even in the city there still is some mud, and there still are some flowers growing in the mud, and some weeds are still down there. He knows the names of the flowers by heart, and so for him to see these flowers growing in the mud takes him outside of what he normally calls himself. There are no windows down by the river, he doesn't look through any window, but there is a membrane there, the membrane between his ordinary world and another world. When he crouches down and touches the petal of a white flower with his fingertip, he enters that other world.

Then, like a door shutting, a sound, say a honking, wakes him, and he turns around, walks back to his car, and drives away from the river. But not away from the other world. He thinks he's left the other world but the other world has come with him, and in fact if he would look in the passenger seat he would see it.

But he's driving now.

Later, at night with his wife . . . No, before that. He's driving his black sedan. He's a doctor making house calls, and he's calling on the sick and dying. Everyone around him is dying and he watches them die, and he knows that death is the end of one world and the beginning of another world and he tries to see what that other world is. He thinks he's standing outside of that other world.

At night, in bed with his wife, with the comforter pulled to their necks, he lies on his back and sees in his mind all the people he's seen dying. Everyone he sees is dying. He looks at his wife and she's dying. He actually sees her skin losing its elasticity and folding into itself like a forgotten piece of fruit.

He knows that death is part of the other world, and he doesn't look at his own face because he knows a person can't live like that. A person can't live in the other world and still live in this one. You start to go crazy. He was starting to see death, or the world of death, and the world of death, which was supposed to stay on its own side, wasn't staying on its own side. It was coming over to his side, and he couldn't live like that.

When they tested the atomic bomb there were men who wanted to see what it looked like with the naked eye and they stood out in front of the shack and watched the explosion. But then they died, because you can't live like that. You have to block it out. Like sunscreen, you have to put up a shield or membrane that keeps that side or that thought or that vision from disrupting what's on this side.

So you try to block it out. But you can't block it out. William Carlos Williams couldn't block it out. He tried not to look at his wife but he dreamed about her. In his dream she was floating facedown on the top of the water. He wanted to wake up but he already was awake. He wanted to stop sweating so he said, "Okay. I don't deny it. It does exist."

"What?" his wife said, waking up. "What's wrong, dear?"

"Nothing."

"There *is* something."

"No," he said. "There's nothing."

"Then why are you looking at me like that?"

If he lived in the other world he couldn't live in this one, and if he didn't live in the other world what was the point of this world? Either way you start to go crazy. He couldn't figure it out. He wanted to be at peace, apparently. Apparently he just wanted that. But this other world had a mind of its own. And it needed things. And the things it needed became the things he needed. But he didn't know what those things were. And if you would have asked him what they were he would've looked at you, but he wouldn't have known what to say.

6

That evening I walked to the yurt where Linda and her friends had been staying. The cars were gone and inside the canvas structure there was just the plywood floor and the empty metal cots. I walked back to the main house, where the party from the night before seemed to have recommenced. I stood on the porch near a plastic tub filled with melted ice. People were walking in and out of the kitchen, standing in groups and playing with dogs. Someone was strumming a guitar.

I saw Feather standing at the edge of the grass, next to a metal support pole, swaying her head to the music. I walked to her, stood beside her, watching her head moving to the music, until she turned around. And when she did, I went from looking at her head to looking into her eyes. I thought that her eyes would turn into Anne's eyes, would speak to me in Anne's voice, but looking into them, I couldn't hear what they were saying.

I'm holding her hand, ready to pull or be pulled, and as people press up against us, and against each other, her hand slips away. I tighten my grip but too late, the hand is gone, and she's gone, and there I am, left with nothing, with no one. And there's a moment of desperation that lasts until, a few moments later, she's back, standing between my hands, hip level, and when I look into *those* eyes, they're different eyes, they're Anne's eyes, and I begin dancing with these eyes. Not dancing, but we move together, pressed against each other.

I didn't drink any punch so I don't know the reason, but dancing like that, and even standing around, later, I was treating her as if she was Anne. We danced some more, got hot, and then we had tequila drinks with ice cubes shaped like the state of Texas. We sat on the steps of the porch, and whatever we talked about must have been preparatory because we stood up at the same time and walked into the house. I followed her into the kitchen, where we stood, holding red plastic cups, not knowing what to talk about, looking at each other, and when I looked at her, when she bent her head, for some reason I kissed her. Or she kissed me.

At any rate we began to kiss, first in the kitchen, and then we went to a little room down the hall. We did all the things we had to do to cross the membrane. I helped her remove her sweater, which got stuck around her wrists, which led to more kissing. I kissed her ears and her full lips. I kissed her neck and when she told me to kiss her stomach I kissed her intertwining arrows. And there must be a million kinds of desire, and we were exploring, through thin cotton material, one of them.

It's hard to experience desire while at the same time controlling it. We were trying to lose control, and when she took my head in her hands we thought we were on our way. We were kissing each other and holding each other and rolling on and off each other, slowly then vigorously, like two too solid worlds trying to come into each other. We were moving purposefully, into and against each other, but nothing seemed to be happening. Nothing was giving way. The thing that should've given way wasn't doing it. She was holding the top of the bed, her eyes falling back into her eyelids, and we were trying to follow our desires, such as we understood them, and we could tell we were close to something, but we weren't breaking through. I with my tongue, and she with her whole damp body, were struggling against some force inside that body, and inside mine, stubbornly blocking access to something we wanted.

140

And what we wanted wasn't bad. But what we needed was something else. I needed to be with Anne and she needed . . . I don't know what she needed but because we wanted a certain experience, and because we felt we were close, we kept working, on and on, and we were feeling sensations, but they were less intense. We felt them, but less so, and then less so, until pretty soon we weren't even doing what we had been doing anymore. We were doing something else. It wasn't bad, but it wasn't what we needed.

We thought maybe we needed to sleep. We were too tired, we thought, or too wide awake, we thought, and maybe we just wanted to go to sleep. We kissed each other, tenderly, like workers coming out of a mine, and then we tried to go to sleep. We thought maybe that was what we needed.

Brigitte Bardot is basically forgotten now, and even in her prime she was notable less for the films she acted in than for the flamboyant sexuality she exhibited in her life. She was, in her time, the symbol of sex, and because she had so much desire, she was also a symbol of that. And why not? Desire had been planted in her—for attention, affection, admiration—and she acknowledged all that and tried to fulfill it, which is why she was famous.

And while those desires were fulfilled, the need she had behind those desires was still there, immanent in the compulsion she felt to keep repeating. Desire exists for itself, in its own delirious state of dissatisfaction. Which is why rich people never have enough money. It's why Brigitte Bardot achieved her reputation, but not the cessation of her desire.

She saw a man and she experienced a feeling that she called desire. That man would soon become her lover. And every time she did this, after a certain time had passed, the desire for that particular person waned. The desire itself was there, but the object of the desire shifted. It seemed to disappear, but when she saw another man, there it was. She felt it again, and she spent years of her life trying to fulfill that feeling.

But the feeling she had existed in a world she was unfamiliar with. She was fulfilling the thing she thought she wanted, but the necessary thing existed in another world.

Feather and I, in our separate worlds, were trying, unsuccessfully, to sleep. We tried to sleep but after a while we realized we weren't sleepy. I certainly wasn't. And thank god for sexual desire because, although she wasn't moving much, everything she did, every in-breath and out-breath, I was aware of. I brushed her hair away and kissed her shoulder, then her back and the soft hairs on the small of her back down to her buttocks, and when she rolled over I kept kissing, and when she tossed her head back and cried out in what's normally called ecstasy, we thought we'd done it.

And we had. We had done it. We felt we'd done the work. But like Brigitte Bardot every time she temporarily eased her desire, we hadn't broken through. We were flushed, our faces were, but we were not completely satisfied. Whatever the necessary thing was, we weren't doing it.

So we stopped. We fell back on the small bed, staring up into the ceiling and feeling the presence of a world we weren't part of.

Then, as if on cue, we both sat up. We sat on the edge of the bed. It was chilly so we covered ourselves with the blanket. We huddled together like that for a long time, looking down at the rug on the floor, and no one said a word.

The two worlds resist coming together, and yet at the same time, there's only one world.

Feather spoke first. She said, "I feel like there's a wall around me."

"A wall of what?" I said.

Our thighs and shoulders were touching, but we weren't looking at each other. "It's glass," she said. "I can see what's out there and hear things, but I can't touch anything, or if I do I'll shatter the glass."

"What would happen if you did?"

"If I shattered the glass? The glass would break."

And that was all we said.

We sat like that a while longer, not speaking. Then we heard some birds outside. And I'm not saying that sitting there we shattered any glass because that would be too dramatic a description of what happened. What happened was that somehow what we wanted and what we needed, for a moment, were the same thing.

7

But then the moment was over and I was back to wanting something else. I'd already gone to another moment, thinking about the possibility of that upcoming moment. However much I tried to accept the moment as it was happening, to twist my mind into the fact of acceptance, I still wanted something else.

By the time I leaned over and kissed Feather on her forehead she was almost asleep. I got dressed, left her in the room, and drove my car into town. I parked on a neighborhood street near a health food store, bought a carrot juice, and spent the rest of the morning sitting in my car, watching the street.

With Anne, I thought, there was love. Not a passing desire, but something solid and true, and thinking this, I realized I hadn't been looking for Anne, not very diligently, and I thought that I should. I thought I ought to make a systematic search of every street in Boulder. But when the morning light brought the people out and onto the street I got out of my car and joined them. I walked along the pedestrian mall, noticing the drains laid in the concrete, and the plants planted in good mulchy soil. I saw the sprinkler heads at the edge of the soil, and I sat on one of the benches, still holding my carrot juice. People were walking by, and I could see that they were noticing me, but mostly they didn't make contact. They kept walking.

I was sitting on this bench in the middle of this pedestrian mall, literally in the center of what would have been a street, but I barely felt that I was there. I was watching the people, who were either watching other people or looking at shoes in the shoe store windows. Right about then a girl sat on the other side of the bench. She had a garbage bag stuffed with laundry and she sat on the bench and we started talking. She had brown hair, tied back, and we talked about New York and deforestation and about hair. I asked her if "brunette" meant the same as brown. We talked about waitressing and copy editing, and at a certain point in the conversation she mentioned that her cat had died. To me it wasn't a monumental problem, but I was thinking that it probably meant something to her, and when she said she needed someone to help bury her cat, I volunteered.

We walked together, up the hill to a lagoon near an official-looking building, a museum or a library, and we stood in front of this lagoon. We were standing there, and I was holding the green plastic garbage bag containing, not her laundry, but her cat. I was about to throw it in the water and I said, "Do you have anything you want to say?" She was wearing a black silk dress from the 1940s, with lace, and a very sensual hat, and she said, "You're the writer, you say something." I didn't even know the cat, and I said, "Well, what was the cat like?" And she said, "That cat had a mind of its own." A mind of its own, I thought, and I said, "Here's to its own mind," and I swung the bag and threw it out into the lagoon. And we watched it. We watched it float. For about fifteen minutes we watched it float out there on the surface of the water and we wanted it to sink, we wanted it to go under the water, but it didn't want that. It wanted to float right where it was. So we didn't know. I found a stick or branch that was lying in the mud and with it, I reached out and pulled the bag back to shore. I untied the knot, folded down the sides, reached in and felt a paw down there. I took hold of the paw, pulled it up, and sure enough, it was a dead cat. I knew it was dead, not because it was stiff, but because it was so still.

145

It was absolutely motionless. It was swaying slightly, but no air was passing in or out, so I kicked the garbage bag out of the way, swung the cat until it got enough momentum, and then threw it back into the lagoon. And we watched it. Again. We watched it keel over to one side and float there on the water. We wanted the cat to sink, but the cat had a mind of its own.

V

Gula

1

I'm driving south, through the Colorado mountains, and although I'm looking for clues, I'm no longer certain that the clues I'm seeing are clues for me. For instance, I'm not sure if the turn signal of the car in front of me is sending me a message to turn or not. Snow-capped mountains are on my right and dry piñon hills are on my left, and when I stop for a barbecue sandwich in a motel town called Buena Vista, the lady in the imitation covered wagon tells me about a hot springs nearby that is supposed to "heal your bones," and I interpret "bones" to mean something unseen inside a person's skin.

That sounds good, so I drive up the alluvial hill, along a winding stream, and find the wind chimes marking the entrance to the hot springs. I drive into the gravel parking lot and it looks like every other two-story motel but this one has water, a series of grotto-like bathing pools set in the hill. People are floating in them, and scattered around the grounds—above the gates and doorways—are hand-painted signs and Indian symbols, reminding visitors of the sanctity of the waters. Peace is infectious, they say, and Listen to the earth.

A pregnant, white-haired girl at the check-in desk tells me that all the rooms in the lodge are taken, but a teepee, she says, is available. So I take my sleeping bag into this teepee, which has a dirt floor, a bunk bed, and a fire pit in the middle. I wash up in the bathroom in the lodge and for about a day my life consists of soaking in the pools of different degrees of heat, floating on foam pads, and at night, more floating, looking up at the stars.

The employees are friendly and healthy, and they all have tattoos or piercings. I talk to a few of them, including the girl from the front desk, who lives in the lodge. She wears loose colorful clothing, and one morning, when the pools are quiet, she offers me a tarot reading. I'm not interested, I say, or ready yet, but after a morning soak I feel comfortable enough to sit with her on the thick red carpeting in the dimly lit recreation room.

Her skin is like slightly tinted milk, her eyes soft, her voice sincere, and sitting on her heels she seems the perfect person to give me some direction, not any direction, but the one direction that will lead me to the reunion with my wife. That she believes she's psychic seems reasonable because everybody seems to be psychic, and maybe everybody is. I tell her a little about myself, tell her my experience so far has been fine but now I want to move on. I say I want to act, and that I'm willing to do it, to see the world with a new view, and because of that new view, be different. I want to fill up the minutes I have with a broader, more inclusive perspective, and that's what I'm doing now. I've never had an aura reading before, never sat cross-legged in a recreation room with a pregnant girl dressed like an Indian who is about to tell me my future.

"Okay," I say.

"Good," she says. She decides we have to move to more private quarters, so we walk out to my teepee. She brings along a candle and some rugs, and she sits at the edge of the fire pit, lighting the candle and placing it in the ashes of the pit. At first I stay perched on the bottom bunk of the bed, watching her preparations, but since she's brought along a rug for me, in the end we both sit, cross-legged, the candle burning between us.

At first she's accurate, talking about loss and tribulation. She tells me I haven't found what I'm looking for, and that to do that, I need a new direction, a direction. So what she's saying, so far, is accurate. When I ask her a more specific question, a question related to Anne, she advises me to move on and forget the past. "The person you're thinking about," she says, "is gone."

Well, at first I refuse to accept that. I ask her what person she's talking about, but I know what person. And it's not that I can't get enough of Anne. She's just there. My thoughts just naturally keep coming back to her, and the girl is suggesting I change my thoughts.

I think about what that might be like. To change my thoughts. And why not? I can exercise a little self-control. When thoughts of Anne start coming to me, I can think of something else. I can notice my thoughts and then change them. I can think about the wind outside the teepee, or the goats I saw that afternoon climbing diagonally up the hillside.

So that's what I do. And it takes some concentration but it works. And because it works I let myself relax. And when I do, every thought that comes to me is a thought of Anne. The happiness I've had with her is a real thing, and every time I think of her, what I feel is the absence in my body. It's painful, but I can't stop it. In the absence of Anne, I manufacture her, and it isn't even an urge, it just happens. My determination to change my mind is overpowered by an urge to maintain the sadness, because that sadness is connected to Anne.

The pregnant girl is telling me about the person she's sensing (Anne), mentioning things I both admire and dislike, telling me that none of it matters because this person is part of the past. As she says this, thoughts, in the form of images, are coming to me. For instance, the time Anne tried to take my photograph. She wanted it to be perfect. She was having trouble with the focus

151

and the light meter, and I saw her desire to succeed. I saw who she was—who she was and what she needed—and I loved who she was. I saw her ambition and her eagerness and her optimism, and I say optimism because optimism was the foundation of our love.

She may or may not have been beautiful, but to me she was beautiful, and what was beautiful was her being. When we love people, what we see are the flaws that make them human. Anne's flaws made our love seem superlative, and I counted myself lucky being in the light of that love. The light was missing now, but as I remembered her, it came back to me. Her uncompromising need for perfection, a trait that at best I put up with, now I longed for. I sat in the teepee, finding Anne in my mind, and liking her there, wondering if maybe I was liking her memory a little too much, but then thinking no, it would probably help. It would probably make it easier to find her if I had her in my mind.

As I did in Cooperstown, New York.

We had taken a trip to the Baseball Hall of Fame, not that you were a baseball fan, but some friends of yours had given us a night at a bed-and-breakfast. There was a snowstorm outside and it was all amazing and wonderful and we never left the room. All that day was spent having sex, until we were numb from it, staying pretty much in or around the bed, eating and making love until, at a certain point, you were complete and I was also complete. We were both empty. And in that long breath of emptiness I felt, not the longing of wanting more, but the peace of wanting nothing.

Of course it wasn't always pleasant. There was that time on Great Jones Street or Bond Street, off Lafayette. We'd gone to a bar after work, with friends, and you were more than a friend at that point but nervous enough about the relationship that you started drinking, we all started drinking, but you kept drinking so that when it was time to leave and we stood on the street, waiting for a cab, you'd left your coat inside. I went back to get it, found it on the floor, and when I brought it out, you were sitting on the curb, bent over, holding your head in your hands and throwing up all over the gutter. I went to you and tried to comfort you, but I didn't know how to do it. I told someone to get some water. I put my hand on your forehead and then you threw up some more. Just an hour earlier you'd been feeling good and you wanted to feel a little more good, but that was too much, that *more* was too much. And now the more was gone. We took a cab home and riding in the cab, looking at your closed eyes, sympathetic or empathetic, I kissed your fore-head which was hot, and your cheeks which were soft and round, and then your lips. I didn't care about anything. I was kissing your mouth because it belonged to you.

All the time I was thinking this, the snowy-haired girl with the loose dress was talking, telling me where I was and what I had to do. She was speaking to me, but I was having a little trouble hearing her. A car was turning out of the parking lot and I was having trouble hearing her because I was paying attention to the shadows of the headlights playing across the canvas skin of the tent. I could see her, a partial silhouette, and I wanted to understand, and because what she was saying was still incom-prehensible, I asked her to repeat.

But it wasn't that I didn't hear her words. I did. And it wasn't that I didn't understand their meaning. She was telling me to let go, and I couldn't let go. I couldn't stop what I was doing because it was what I had to do.

And of course I had reasons, in my mind, to discount what she was telling me. She was just a twenty-some-year-old imitation

153

Indian shaman who didn't know enough of life to tell me that my life, with my wife, was over.

And yet I suspected that she was probably right.

On the one hand I had a mind of my own, and on the other hand I had another mind, and I seemed to be somewhere between the two.

2

I could soak only so long, and once I'd left the thermal springs motel all I really remembered about the white-haired psychic girl was that she wore an Indian outfit and Indian jewelry. That became the clue, and as I drove out of the green valleys of Colorado and into the red canyons of the West, I was glad, first of all, to be moving, and second to be moving toward something vaguely Indian, and through that vague something Indian, to Anne.

Around midday I found a monument marker indicating an Indian cliff-dwelling site. I'd already driven past several Indian information centers, but something about the layout of the parking lot convinced me to stop. I immediately noticed the dry, quiet air. The sandstone walls rising up on either side of the canyon were streaked with red. I began hiking down the steps made of railroad ties, into a riverbed with cottonwood and chaparral and piñon pine. I wanted to see no people (meaning no white people) because I wanted to see and hear only what the ancient people who lived here had to tell me. This was their place and I didn't know how they would speak to me but I was listening. To the birds flitting from branch to branch and the slow-moving stream. Even the delicate clouds, evaporating in the heat of the sun, seemed to be speaking.

Keet Seel is one of the more out-of-the-way cliff dwellings in northern Arizona, and I was alone when I got to the actual cliff, to the city that once existed in that cliff. The dwellings were made from the same red stone, built in the hollow where the cliff had fallen away, and now they were part of the cliff. I could see the actual mud mortar holding the buildings together, and I imagined the life of this village as it was when it was still alive, the women getting water, the men in their leather moccasins, not taking more than they needed, living with scarcity rather that constantly filling themselves with stuff. I was trying to make these dwellings in the desert stand for civilization or the effects of greed on civilization, but these people weren't greedy. And yet at some point in the middle of their history they disappeared, and now even the remains of that history were crumbling back into the earth.

As I walked up a slope of fallen stone and adobe, I saw at the bottom of the talus, mixed in with the rubble, a small flat piece of something in the dirt. I picked it up. It was a piece of pottery, some part of a clay vessel with black and dark red markings, mostly worn away. I looked at the markings, just a couple of dark lines and a part of a triangle shape, and I held this clue like a talisman. With it I began searching for other shards that might fit together with my shard and make some sense. I was down on my hands and knees sifting through the rough red sand, holding my shard in one hand, digging with the other.

And then I heard a voice coming from somewhere in the dwelling above me. I followed the sound of the voice up into the first level of the building. I entered a miniature doorway at the base of the structure. I could see pieces of wood sticking out of the adobe walls; there was a ladder made of well-worn tree limbs. I climbed that and emerged in an open area. A round uncovered kiva was to my right and I didn't climb any farther because I didn't want to wear away the adobe. But I listened and as I listened I heard the voice, this time behind me. I turned, and the ranger, a woman ranger, was standing there.

"What's that?" she said.

She was referring to the shard in my hand, the shard I'd found, and having found it, I wanted to keep it. I didn't want to let go of it. I thought about running, that I could probably outrun the ranger, but then what? I'd have my piece of pottery but then what?

The ranger was tan, wearing sunglasses. I stepped forward and presented her with my piece of pottery.

And that was that. Until later, when I walked back to my car. I stopped at the trailhead, near some cottonwoods, and as I stood on the sand by the barely moving stream, I imagined that no more shards would ever be found, that my shard was the last shard and now it was gone and I'd never see it again. I wished I had looked at it more carefully. If only I'd had a little more time with the shard, maybe I could have deciphered what it meant, and what it might have meant to me if it were still mine.

3

I was traveling on the small roads now, meandering as much as I could so as to miss as little as possible. The hills of central Arizona aren't treacherous, but some of them are steep, and I was winding my way up one of the steeper ones when I noticed the car starting to stall. Maybe it was the high altitude, or I was low on gas, or the engine was hot. Whatever it was, although it was sputtering, it didn't die, and I made it to the top of the hill, to an Indian casino, and pulled into the parking area.

Inside the casino the air conditioning was going full blast, and I sat down at a slot machine, and since I had a few quarters I started to play. Each time I played I had hope. Each time I lost, a new hope took its place. My losing continued and it wasn't even luck anymore, it was mathematics, probability, and because I had to be rewarded at some point I waited for the pictographs in the machine to come into a line. I said to myself I would leave when I won, and I was waiting for that to happen.

The casino was lit in a way that made it seem both dark and bright, and there was a lot of blinking and sounds, and I was slightly lost in my excitement, waiting to hit it big. And of course the big payoff never came. I walked back out to the parking lot, having lost some of my precious money, and feeling sick almost from my overindulgence, I got in the car. As I made the right turn out of the casino, on the way down the hill, the car engine stopped. It just stopping going. I felt it had something to do with that casino, or the corruption of the traditional

Indian way of life, but it didn't matter because the car was dead. I should say the engine was dead because the car itself hadn't stopped moving. It was going down the hill and the wheels of the car didn't know anything was wrong, they kept moving, and I coasted along, all the way down to a town at the bottom of the hill. As I turned a corner the car slowed and settled to a stop in front of a real estate office.

The car sounded, when I tried to start it, as if gas wasn't getting to the engine. Pushing the pedal did nothing. A man coming out of the office directed me to an auto parts store and the man there told me to test the fuel filter by blowing through it to see if it was clear. And when I took off the old filter and couldn't blow through it, I bought a new one. With a screwdriver and a pair of pliers I replaced the clogged fuel filter, but when I tried to start the car, it didn't do any good.

A car-repair shop was visible at one end of the town, and when the traffic along the two-lane main street had passed, I pushed the car across the road and down to where the broken cars were parked. Fortunately for me, the Pulsar was a subcompact, and by standing at the open driver's-side door, I could push and steer at the same time, which I did. A man in overalls told me it would take three days to fix, so I walked down the street to another place, where a guy named Larry suggested what might be the problem. Fuel pump, he said, which was a major repair, or major enough, because by this time I was beginning to be concerned about my dwindling supply of money. I still had credit cards, but because I wanted to conserve my resources, even though he told me it was imperative to repair the problem, I did something else.

I bought a Gatorade at a main-street market. I looked around at the pine-tree mountains, and after I drank my drink, the car, for some reason, started. I drove to Larry, who seemed like a compassionate mechanic. He found part of a broken vacuum tube that was causing the car to stall and he glued it together with epoxy, for free.

As I drove out of town, up through the switchback mountains, the landscape got prettier and greener, and I was hoping my car difficulties were over. I was tired of difficulties, tired of the stress on my system, and to relieve the stress, when I came upon a crater lake I pulled into the parking lot. It was a green lake with rock outcroppings around the edges, and I stood at the viewpoint and looked at the lake, and when I went back to the car it didn't start. I was thinking I should have left it running, but my habit now was to wait a few minutes and try again, and after a few minutes of waiting, sure enough, it started.

Continuing along toward Flagstaff, I saw a congregation of people on the side of the road. The sun was setting and the people were watching, off in the distance, a herd of elk ranging in a green river meadow. People were looking through binoculars and so I pulled over, took out my worthless antique binoculars, and of course couldn't see anything through the clouded glass, but as I was looking, the car stopped running. A man leaning against a pickup truck offered to help. He said he knew something about cars, and after reaching under the hood, he told me there was something clogging the fuel line, some particle of dirt or carbon, and he suggested I fix it immediately.

The man followed me along for a while but I was fine. I waved him on. Every time I was about to stall I would shift into neutral, and in this way I drove into Flagstaff, to the area where the automotive repair shops were. They were already closed for the day, so I spent the night in the car on a side street.

I spent the next day talking with mechanics in Flagstaff, starting with an Indian guy who was working at Bill's on Route 66. Then the Nissan place, which was expensive. An old man in front of a discount store told me to put cleaning solvent in the gas tank and carburetor. Which I did. But as I drove up the hill leading out of town it stalled again, this time in the middle of a busy road, and so I found a long-haired kid mechanic who said something about a new air cleaner. I went to an educated mechanic, who sent me to a hairy mechanic, who sent me to a mad scientist mechanic. But because the trouble I was having was transitory, because when they looked at the car everything seemed to be functioning, none of them could help.

And the reason I didn't leave the car with these mechanics had something to do with the price they'd be charging, and something to do with risk. There was a pleasure in pushing my luck. And it wasn't that I was enjoying the car trouble, but I was becoming used to it, almost addicted to it. The car trouble was distracting me from something else, which had nothing to do with the car, but the car was what I was focusing on.

4

It was late afternoon when I drove out of Flagstaff, and when I turned off the road, I thought I was turning into the sacred Wupatki Pueblo National Monument, but I ended up instead turning into the Sunset Crater National Monument. Since it was getting close to sunset, instead of reading any informational literature, I decided to sit on a rock and have a picnic. I was eating an apple, looking at the slanting light hit the rocks, and the shadows of the rocks, and for the first time in a long time I felt a degree of peace. The twisted wood of the shrub conifers, and the wind-carved stone, and the warmth still emanating off the earth. Something about the warmth was melting something in me, and I ate the apple, relishing its crunch. I threw the core into a waste container and for a long time just stood, listening to the distant hum of traffic, and the birds, closer, and the wind on my face. The smell of the dry dirt, and the dry air, and the horizon, stretching my eyesight and stretching itself, into the distance.

When another car pulled into the overlook and several children jumped out I decided to get moving. There was a loop drive that wound through the park and I was going to drive along that until I found another spot where I could survey the scenery. As I drove, the sky was taking on the reddish glow of the beginning of sunset, and I was looking out at that, driving down the gentle grade, my body alive in the seat, and I wouldn't have admitted it, but I was imagining myself as an early human inhabitant.

Then came a swoosh sound and the engine stopped running. The car continued to coast down the hill and I let it coast, the engine quiet, the valley in front of me. When I came to a stop at the bottom of the hill, I pulled off the road again, got out again, and opening the hood again, I felt, perhaps, that my car was telling me something. About where I was. And I didn't mind being where I was. But I couldn't stay there, not really, so I started the car, or tried to. I waited the requisite minutes and tried, but the car didn't start. Not only that, but it didn't have the familiar sound of *trying* to start. It was a lifeless wheezing, and it worried me a little. But I waited again and tried again, jiggling wires and trying over and over, removing and replacing the fuel filter and trying again, and every time I tried, nothing happened.

The sky, which had been becoming dark, now *was* dark, and there I was, on the side of the road, and just about when I was thinking of spending the night where I was a car drove by. I flagged it down and the man who was driving came over and looked at the Pulsar. He had a flashlight and he shined it at an area to the side of the engine block. He said it was the timing belt, or timing chain—he said it was known by both—and that it wasn't turning. This was serious, he said.

And as this man, a photographer, was pronouncing the car in big trouble, a truck drove up with men in the back, Hopi men, who lived near there and worked for the park and were going home. They looked at the car too, and they agreed that the timing chain was a serious problem. If it *was* the problem. The photographer reminded me that you never knew how bad it was until the engine was taken apart. They all helped push the car back onto a small dirt road, and since it was night by now and where to go was an issue, Gilbert, the Hopi man driving the truck, told me I'd better come with him.

When he said this, and when he had earlier agreed to the timing chain theory, he didn't use many words. He said what he had to say and then he was quiet. The photographer drove off and I got in the back of the truck with three other Indian men, all wearing cowboy boots, and during the drive I didn't talk. Once I asked one of the men if it was dangerous in the desert at night, but all the man did was nod. We drove on an old rutty road for about twenty minutes, the men in the back getting off at various roads in the dirt until at the end it was just Gilbert and me when we pulled into a kind of compound.

There were several dogs barking and some children near the house. It was a small house and modern, or fairly modern, built in a conventional way. Not far off was another building, a six-sided hogan with a sod roof. Gilbert went into the regular house and I started to follow. First I looked up into the night sky, which was black except for the stars, and then I followed Gilbert inside.

A woman was doing something at a stove and an older woman was sitting on a rocking chair. The older one was wearing a deep green shirt and a long full ruffled skirt. No one said anything to anyone as far as I could tell. Gilbert sat at a square table and I also sat and still no one spoke.

Gilbert nodded when I thanked him for the ride. I asked some question about sheep and whether he had any sheep and he pointed in a general direction with his hand. I nodded. I had so much to tell them, to share with them in words, but I could see that words were not the medium here, and in living without the gluttony of words, they were taking the burden off the descriptions of things and letting the things themselves be what they were. Although these people weren't speaking, I imagined that when they did, their words would be a little purer and a little more meaningful.

I assumed that not speaking was a normal mode of relating and so I stopped trying to speak, stopped trying to think of something to say, and instead just sat. The fact that everyone else was doing the same thing made it easier. We all sat for quite a while and it didn't take too long before it felt normal, and even comfortable.

The woman was making food, and food, I thought—that would be a good way to bond with this family. I was starting to feel at home in this strange abode. And happy. And because I wanted that feeling to last (into the future), I began wondering where I was going to sleep, thinking I should have brought my sleeping bag because I didn't see any extra beds, and as my mind raced ahead, I was looking forward to sleeping in the traditional Navajo dwelling. Or Hopi dwelling, I didn't know.

Either way, it was a memorable experience, one I would savor and cherish, and as I was thinking about what a fine experience it was and how happy the experience was making me, a car drove up outside. Gilbert went to the door and there, standing at the door, was a white man, a ranger. He'd seen the Pulsar, he said, and now he was here to take me back—something about the native domiciles being off-limits, or private property, or National Park regulations. My car, however, was a unique situation, and so he'd make an exception and let me spend the night in my car. I nodded at Gilbert, who nodded back, and I got in the truck with the ranger. He dropped me off, took down my information, said he'd check back in the morning and that I could make the necessary arrangements then to have my car towed out of the park.

The stars were out and then the clouds came in and I stood outside, leaning against the car. I drank from a bottle of water, ate cashews, unrolled my sleeping bag in the back seat, and although I tried to sleep, I was awake the whole night. My mind was filled with thought after thought, starting with the car. Why hadn't I fixed the car before it was ruined? Why had I been such a cheapskate? And it wasn't the car; it was my life. The dream I'd had for my life was getting smaller and smaller, shrinking and cracking, and at a certain point tears actually came to my eyes. I was crying for that dream, or the loss of that dream. I felt an actual physical pain, a heaviness in my body. And once I felt it, once the reality of the deadness of my dream started festering in me, sleep was impossible.

5

I mentioned that I was an editor in New York, at a baby magazine. But I wasn't always an editor. Growing up in Chicago I had, I don't know what to call it, a dream, I guess. I wanted to be a playwright. I felt I needed an identity, as a person. I needed something I could be, some thing, and I thought a playwright, that was something I could be, I could live with that. If I was a playwright I could be happy, I thought, so I got together with some people and started a theater company. I did all the things I thought a playwright would do. I got an odd job. I wrote a play. I wrote this play and the play got a production and I thought, Okay, this is it, I will be the thing I want to be. This will make me what I want to be, I thought, and the theater mounted the play and the play was a failure, critically and artistically. I could see that. But I thought, No, you learn from your mistakes. Yes, you do, you learn, and I did, I learned from my mistakes and I knew, I knew what to do the next time. I wrote another play, and this play was much more original. It was something no one had ever seen before, and it was going to blow the walls away. I directed it, with a pornographic movie projected on a screen behind the actors, and I thought it would be good, really good, and I was excited about it. But the play was a failure. A different kind of failure, but a failure nonetheless. But no, I thought, you learn from your mistakes, yes, yes you do, and not only that but those obstacles make you stronger. A great playwright isn't just born, you have to struggle and overcome the obstacles and be stronger, and I was, I was getting better. I knew what I'd been doing wrong. So I wrote another play, and I thought this play would be good, and it was, it was really good, it was from a true-life experience and it really was good and this play won a prize. So the confidence I had in myself was confirmed, by an outside source, and yes, I thought, I'm on my way to being the thing I want to be. I'll be happy now. And that's great, and the play won another prize. I was flown to New York and I thought, Okay, here we go, and I felt as if the world . . . here it is, and I went to New York and the New York producers looked at it and it wasn't quite right for them, they said. But that was okay because a theater was planning a Chicago production, and I thought, That's good, that's better, start small, start small and then just go forward, conquer the world, and the theater put on the show and no one came and the show lost a lot of money. The theater company went bankrupt, and I didn't know what to do. I began to think, Something is not right here, obviously, and I took some time off and I discovered what it was, what it was I wasn't doing. I wasn't being myself. I was trying to do something else, and that's it, I thought, I will write a play that is who I am, about people and the things between people, and the society, and the structure of that society. And I wrote this play that I thought was good, brilliant even, and it had a reading and it was terrible. It was. I was cringing at my own words. And so I didn't know. I just didn't know. And I began to think that maybe the dream was not the right dream. Maybe I had the wrong dream. But I didn't want to say that, I didn't want to admit defeat. I was strong. I could persevere. And I was walking along, in New York, on Wooster Street, it was Wooster Street because the sidewalk was bumpy and I had to keep my eyes down so as not to trip, and I was walking along, and all of a sudden I felt it snap. It snapped. The dream. The dream died. And I let it die. It didn't feel that bad. In fact it felt good. It felt like what it must feel like, or what I imagined it must feel like, when a dream comes true.

6

In the morning the ranger knocked on my window. He gave me
a ride to the ranger station where I called the towing service.
As I waited for the tow truck, I wandered around the exhibits
and dioramas, reading about desert plants. As I sat on the toilet
in the Park Service headquarters I realized I hadn't thought
about Anne for almost a day, and thinking that, I remembered
how she used to arch her feet when she sat on the toilet.

When the tow truck came I watched the man hook the Pulsar
to a chain and winch it onto the truckbed. I got in the cab and
we drove off across the undulating flatness of the desert, punctuated here and there by masses of less eroded sandstone in the
otherwise eroded expanse. There were ruins along the road but
I wasn't paying all that much attention. I was worried about the
bill. The driver, the son of the tow truck owner, talked about
timing belts and said there was a fifty-fifty chance of piston
damage.

We pulled into the Sinagua Trading Post, a curio shop and
towing service with a junkyard in the back. It was run by a man
named Cecil, an old Arizona leatherneck—literally a man with
a leatherlike neck—who told me my car was junk. He said he'd
fix it if I wanted him to, but there was a fifty-fifty chance of
valve damage. He said he'd buy the car and offered me fifty
dollars, which just about covered the tow.

I wanted more than that. This was my life and I didn't want
to *give* it away, which is what the man, essentially, was asking.

I was not in a good negotiating position, leverage-wise, but I didn't want to let go. I'd bought the car and had invested the car with my dreams. Money too, but mainly dreams. I'd invested that small, powerless, uncomfortable car with my life, so it wasn't that easy to just let go, to just say *Take it*, to just walk away from what had been my self.

When we dream of cars and driving in cars, they say we're dreaming, partly, about our selves, the things that move us through the world. And at first Cecil seemed to recognize this; he was polite and even compassionate, but he was also businesslike. He added up the hours replacing a timing belt, and parts. Plus the tow. Plus the fact that the car wasn't worth that much from the get-go. And then he gave me time to think. Which I did, outside the store, on a bench in the shade, looking at the hills, watching cars pass on the road. Slowly I came to a realization that the era of the car—and me in the car—was over. My car was gone, and being gone it was one less thing to stuff my life with.

So I sold the car. In the process of selling it, what with papers of transfer and registration fees, I ended up having to pay Cecil (with my credit card) about fifty dollars, but it was worth it. I felt a lightness. I'd lost this thing which had meant so much to me and now, without it, I felt a weight had been lifted. Instead of feeling the loss I thought I would feel, I felt renewed.

I took the cactus out of the car, carried it to a suitable location in the desert sand, dug a shallow hole with my fingers, and planted it. I left the antique binoculars in the glove compartment, and I took out of the car my box of books and the envelope of photographs, including the one which had fallen off the dashboard. I took my laptop computer, the plastic sack of cassette tapes, the mandolin, a backpack filled with my clothes and sleeping bag, and a small red shoulder bag. I stood in the sun, in front of the building's Fort Apache architectural façade, and once again I was waiting. This time for a ride into town where I would catch a bus, somewhere.

After a while of waiting, a man in a large mobile home who'd stopped at the trading post gave me a ride. He was a retiree who told me that "Anasazi" was no longer a correct term for the ancient people who lived there. He said that "Anasazi" meant "enemy" in Navajo, and that the Hopi, who also lived in the area, naturally thought the word was an incorrect description. People had lived with the word for a long time, but now, according to the man, quoting a Visitor Center brochure, they were changing it.

The man let me off at a main intersection in the northern part of Flagstaff, near the railroad depot. I was going to do what people do in the movies, take the first train out of town, but a railroad employee in a booth told me no train was leaving anywhere until the next day, and since it was already getting into the afternoon, I started walking to one of the bars the man recommended, walking with my box of books in my arms, the backpack and haversack and mandolin on my shoulders, and the bag of cassettes in my fingers, until my fingers gave out, then stopping, setting down the load, resting, then walking some and then resting, then walking and resting, and I carried my possessions into an older, seedier quarter where I happened to see the El Rancho Grande, a bar I'd noticed the day before. It was an old bar, an old-style bar, almost empty, and I went to the bar and took the money I had left and had a beer. I was leaning against the bar in a typical way when an older woman who looked a little ragged took the stool next to me, said "Hi," and then asked me to buy her a drink. Which I did. She introduced herself as Conchita, which was fine, but then from somewhere in the shadows of the bar another woman, a younger woman, joined me on the other side. This was Conchita's niece, named Cheyenne, and she also wanted a drink.

I said I really didn't have enough money, which was mostly true, but I also wanted to start on my new life and I wasn't sure this was it. I wanted to be rid of unnecessary appurtenances, but money was not, at this point, unnecessary. I said I couldn't buy them a drink but I offered to go in on a pitcher of beer, but by then they were already kneeling on the floor, examining the plastic bag filled with cassette tapes.

I offered them my books. I said, "Check out some of these," but they were too busy checking out the tapes. I'd spent years recording the songs on those tapes but I was ready to let them go. My new friends weren't impressed with my taste in music but they wanted the tapes, and were reaching into the plastic sack, indiscriminately taking every tape that touched their hands, not that they intended to listen to them, but because these things existed. I told them to take the whole bag, which they did, too far gone, or too lost in their own wanting, to notice when I left.

Although my load was somewhat lighter, I still had the other articles of my life, and I carried these up the street to a coffee shop. The train depot worker had mentioned a "hangout" place, and this was it. An imitation New York beatnik coffeehouse. I noted the college students sitting at various secondhand tables, and I was going to order something warm and comforting, but realized that I was extremely low on money. So I just sat at the wooden bar. Someone sat down next to me, a student probably, and this person started talking to me. She looked like a student and I talked to her, and oddly, I didn't want to sleep with her, which would have also meant a place to stay. Instead, I asked her if she liked to read books.

She said she did and I showed her the ones in my box and she picked out a couple that interested her. I pointed out the mandolin case and she opened it, took out the instrument, and although she said she couldn't play, she held it as if she was about to play. I told her it was my father's mandolin and that I couldn't play it.

"You can have it," I said, but she said she didn't need it. "I would like you to have it," I said, and she took it and thanked me. She held it flat in her arms. I showed her the computer in my backpack. "Are you kidding?" she said. "It's old," I said, and I set it on top of the mandolin case. She stood there. "I don't know," she said, and I told her, "I'm not using it anymore."

I wanted to give away the ache in my heart, and I was hoping that if I unburdened myself of my possessions the ache would go away. She agreed to take the computer and the mandolin, and I ended up leaving the box of books on the floor, in front of a glass display of muffins and scones.

She led me to a table where her friends were sitting. She had me take a seat and offered me a cigarette from one of the packs on the table. A half dozen people were sitting around the table, talking about a potato gun someone had made that shot potatoes into the air, and they were laughing about this, and all the time the talk was going on I could hear them, and I could see them, but a veil was placed between me and them. It seemed. I was in the circle, at the table, but at the same time I was removed from the circle. I was receding even as they spoke to me. Even as I answered their questions and commented and laughed, I was fading, and I could feel myself fade, and I didn't like it. Partly I *did* like it. Partly, I felt serene in this state. Serene and numb.

But I was only numb and serene on the outside. Inside, in with my organs of memory, I was in another state, and it was in this state that I thought about what had happened at the gas station in New Jersey. The people at the table were talking away, happy and convivial, and it wasn't that I wanted to think about a time in the past. I wanted to be done with the past, but I could hear the dark car and the brakes of the dark car right before it collided with our little maroon car.

Anne had stopped to pick me up from the convenience store entrance. I was just getting into our car, just opening the door, and that's when I heard the brakes, and in a split second I looked up, saw the outline of darkness. And I felt the impact. Anne was hurt. They had collided with her side of the car and I was all right but Anne was knocked forward into the window and the steering column and she wasn't speaking. She was unconscious. The dark car sped off and I tried to look at the license plates but I was more concerned with Anne. I went to her, held her head in my hands, and something was wrong. I told someone to call an ambulance and I didn't know what to do. I didn't want to slap her and there was no doctor. I asked for a doctor but it was just the gas attendants and they didn't know anything. No one knew anything and I didn't either. She was dying. I didn't know. What it meant. She was breathing. I felt a pulse but I couldn't wake her up. When finally the ambulance came I was yelling at them, why it took so long, and they didn't want me in the back. I wanted to be in the back with Anne but they wouldn't let me and so I had to find them later, had to find the hospital, they took her to a hospital in New Jersey. I didn't know New Jersey. I knew Mount Sinai but that wasn't in New Jersey and they told me which one but I didn't know where it was and the car wasn't working and I wanted to be with Anne. I wanted to be with Anne. I kept telling them that I wanted to be with my wife.

7

There I was, walking through the night, but even with my lighter
load, the feeling of lightness had slipped away. Carrying only
my small backpack, containing everything that was mine, I
walked through the night, walking south, down the nearest road,
not because I wanted to go in that direction, but because that
was the road I was already on. I felt I couldn't stop moving,
that I had to keep moving. I felt that if I didn't keep moving
I'd fall, like a child on a bicycle.

I was walking past gas stations and fast-food outlets, walking
and turning and putting out my thumb, when a car passed. And
the cars did pass, and they didn't stop, and after a while I found
myself walking through a temporary city, a temporary-looking
city, built with trailers and aluminum siding, and the parking
lots weren't paved. There were bars and stores and trucks parked
at these establishments but no sense of solidity. I walked into
a go-go nightclub to see if I could find someone going my way
and maybe get a drink of water. I wanted to save my money
and since just to sit in a chair cost money I walked back out
into the night and the temporary town gave way to cleared land,
newly plowed and leveled earth, drained of color and ready for
development, ready for money to be made. I walked past irri-
gation ditches and rows of trees, and then like a nomad coming
to a palm oasis, I came to an area of palm trees. Palm trees and
green grass. Even in the night I could see it was green. The
houses weren't houses exactly, but they were meant to be lived

176

in. They were all model homes, extremely suburban model townhomes, made to look like chalets, and the streets were winding, not because they had to be, but because it was someone's vision. This was a manufactured town. A faux town. It was also deserted, which was good for me because now I could sleep. I found an area of sand, a children's play area near some green grass, and because I wanted to stay dry, I lay in the sand, away from the sprinklers that seemed to go on at irregular intervals. I lay in the sand waiting to fall into a deep, deep sleep because soon it would be morning.

And then it *was* morning.

I left the children's playground before the security guards would make their rounds, and continued walking. I was headed in a definite direction. I needed a direction and I had it. And this feeling of direction I had was confirmed, I thought, when I walked to the highway and the first vehicle driving along the road, or almost the first vehicle, a truck with a Mexican driver, gave me a ride to Phoenix, Arizona.

Phoenix was named after a place named after a bird that rises from the ashes, and I found a quiet corner at a Winchell's coffee shop, where I sat over coffee near a group of old men, the old men of Phoenix, who were talking about dead friends and dying friends, and I sat there, blending in with the bright, unobtrusive surroundings.

It seemed strange to me that whenever I thought of Anne I automatically felt despair. And the strange thing was, I felt the most despair when I thought of our happiest moments. You'd think that the happy moments would have engendered pleasant feelings, but instead I felt almost dead.

When I say "almost dead" I mean that, although I'd rid myself of some possessions, I needed to get rid of more, needed to rid myself of the habit of being what I was. Since I knew

177

about a hypnotist who lived in Phoenix, Arizona, and since I was now in Phoenix, Arizona, I went to see this hypnotist. I didn't have an appointment, I just went to the man's house. I found the address in the telephone book and walked past the cacti in his front yard and stood at his screen door, listening. I could hear a television show going on inside. It was *Bewitched*, a show in which Darrin, the husband, wants Samantha, the witch, his wife, to renounce her magical abilities. She doesn't totally understand why he would want her to keep these powers, which are completely natural to her, in check. But she was willing to try, willing to accommodate him, and she was trying. Then a commercial came on and I was thinking I should knock on the door because the man would know, by the sounds of the birds, or the absence of the sounds of the birds, or some sense perception I wasn't privy to, that I was standing on the other side of the screen.

So I knocked, and the man called out for me to come in. He was sitting in a wheelchair and I squatted beside him and we started talking. He was what I would have called a kindly old man, and he asked me what I wanted. I didn't tell him about Anne, but I told him I wanted some direction. "There are a lot of directions," he said. "But if you're standing on the North Pole there's only one." He showed me his collection of carved animals and said that I wasn't an Indian. "But," he said, "if you want to be hypnotized, come back in an hour."

So I went back in an hour, not to his house, but next door, to his small office. He greeted me and indicated that I should sit in a comfortable chair facing the window. He wheeled his wheelchair opposite me so that as I looked out, the window framed his head, and while he was talking he was asking me what I wanted him to talk about. I was going to tell him that I wanted him to talk about the unconscious part of my mind. I was going to tell him that I thought my unconscious mind might have something to tell me. I was going to tell him that I was afraid of the unconscious mind, afraid of the loss of consciousness, but he kept talking.

He was talking about something, very slowly, saying things that I was listening to, and hearing, and watching. The man's head was shifting positions in front of the window and I began feeling my own head, not shifting, but wondering, was I moving my head because the man was, or was the man moving because I was? The window also seemed to be moving, or vibrating, and I was thinking about the silhouette of the man's head touching the edges of the window, and also about the time, years ago, at a place called The Chuck Wagon.

I'd been with Anne, on a vacation. We'd gone to a theater or club above a restaurant called The Chuck Wagon, where a hypnotist named Dr. Dean put on a kind of show, an exhibition of hypnotic phenomena. Because I wanted to experience hypnosis, when Dr. Dean asked for volunteers, I went up on the stage with all the other people, sat in a chair in a row and I tried to see Anne in the audience, but it was dark and the lights were shining in my eyes. Dr. Dean began talking, not to the volunteers, but to the audience. He was facing the volunteers, moving his arms up and down, in his black suit, moving his arms and telling the audience what the people on stage were supposed to do, which was to breathe, which they all did. The people on stage began dropping off. He was telling them to go to sleep. And people were doing it. But I wasn't doing it. I wanted to. Some part of me wanted to drop right off with the rest of them, to believe that I could, but it wasn't happening. But I wanted it to happen. So what I did was fake it. I was good at pretending and so I pretended it happened. I relaxed my head like the man in front of me and let it fall to my chest. But because I wasn't really sleeping I had to keep watching the man in front of me to see if I was doing whatever it was they were all doing, to see if I was doing it right. It was like looking in a mirror. I could see myself only when I was looking at myself. The minute I turned away . . .

Dr. Dean is saying, "Go down, down, all the way down." And that's what I am trying to do. I'm trying to do that but there's a gulf between wanting and doing, and on one side are the cliffs of wanting and on the other side are the cliffs of doing, and I'm in the middle, I'm the river, except I'm not flowing, I'm just sitting there. I'm not bridging that gulf. And Dr. Dean knows that. He begins pointing to some of the volunteers, telling them to go back to their seats. "You and you and you." And then he points to me. He pauses. "You almost made it."

Then I heard the old man saying, "Open your eyes."

I don't know what he's talking about. "They're already open," I tell him.

"Of course they are," he says. "Any fool can see that." He wheels his wheelchair over to the door and for some reason I think this is very funny. I can feel a huge grin forming on my face. And the man is smiling too, we're both smiling, and it's very funny. But I don't know what it is. I know I'm smiling but I don't know why. I try to think, Why am I smiling?

The man looks up from his wheelchair. "It's easy to move your mouth in a certain way. It's easy to do many things." He looks toward the door, and still smiling, I stand up, I thank the man, and then I walk out the door.

VI

Acedia

1

The gas station in New Jersey. There we were. We'd been talking, happy and convivial. Anne was getting gas and I'd gone into the store to get some snacks for the trip. As I came out of the store she was waiting at the entrance, and I was just about to open the door of the car when that other car . . . I didn't see it but I could hear the dark car, and the brakes of the dark car, as it collided with our little station wagon. Anne had parked, not in the road, because there wasn't an actual road, but on the asphalt, and she was waiting, the car running, and I was just opening the door, just starting to get into the car, and that's when I heard the brakes, looked up, and for a split second I saw the outline of darkness that was that other car colliding with our car, with the driver's side of our car. I was all right but Anne was knocked forward into the window and the steering column and she wasn't speaking. She was unconscious. The dark car sped off and I tried to see the license plates but I was more concerned with Anne. I went to her, held her head in my hands, and something was wrong. She was hurt, I told someone to call an ambulance. I didn't know what to do. I didn't want to slap her and there was no doctor. I asked for a doctor but there were just the gas station attendants and they didn't know anything. No one knew anything and I didn't either. Was she dying? I didn't know. She was breathing, and I could feel a pulse, but I couldn't wake her up. When finally the ambulance came I was yelling at them, why it took so long, and they let me ride in the back, on a bench, and there was another man, a medic of some sort, and he'd made a bag of liquid that he attached to a tube that went into her arm. I wanted to look at her and see her but this man put a mask over her face, to help her breathe or make her breathe, and there were bumps on the road and the siren was going but I didn't hear it. The man didn't talk and I didn't talk, not to him. I told Anne to be all right, to feel fine, and her eyes were closed except for a brief flash. She opened them, looked up, and I was there so she saw me. And then she didn't. And we got to the hospital and they slid her out and wheeled her into the emergency part of the hospital and I was left outside a door. They took her through this door and I waited to see her. I wanted to be with her. I wanted to see her but I never did. Not alive. That brief look was all I got. And then she was dead. After that my Anne was dead.

2

So here I am. So okay. Man of adjustment and all that. So what do I do? There's nothing I can do.

I look around.

I happen to be standing by a light pole, bleached by the sun, in a town (Gila Bend) that could hardly be called a town, and wouldn't be except for the several gas stations and the bend in the road. I too am bleached, standing without sunblock, without direction, and also without the belief I'd spent so much time believing. If my world was one thing, and now that world is gone, there's still a world, but it's not my world anymore, and certainly not a world I care very much about. I still exist, still have what seems like existence, but the reason for moving is gone. So I'm not moving. I'm not hitchhiking, not walking, not watching the occasional passing car. I'm just standing there, between two nearly identical gas stations, one red, one green. And that's when a white sedan pulls up along the shoulder on the road, ahead of where I'm standing. I don't know if the car is stopping for me, or for some internal reason that has nothing to do with me, but when I walk to the car, the car doesn't drive away. I look in the open window and there's an old man, healthy but old, looking at me.

"Where are you going?" he says.

"Yuma," I say, pulling a random name off my memory of the map.

"That's where I'm going," the man says.

I throw my bag in the back seat, get in the front, and off we go. There's some minor chitchat as we drive across the burnt flat desert but the man doesn't spend much time beating around the bush. After only a couple of miles he asks me if I would like to have my dick sucked. I decline, as politely as possible, and that's about it until the man casually mentions that he's not really going to Yuma, that in fact he's getting off at the next exit.

"You said you were going to Yuma," I remind him.

"That was a mistake."

"What do you mean mistake?" I say. "You said you would take me to Yuma."

"I could," the man says, and leaves the rest of his thought just dangling.

Then, holding the steering wheel with one hand, he reaches over to the glove compartment and takes out a round piece of plastic. He puts this plastic to his mouth and begins talking, pretending that he's talking to some other car, as if the piece of plastic is a radio, a wireless radio, and he begins asking if there's anyone on the road going to Yuma. Then he places this object, a brown piece of Bakelite, against his ear and cocks his head as if listening. After a pause he tells me that there's a car behind us going to Yuma and that the driver is willing to give me a ride.

"Are you kidding?" I say. "What are you trying to do?"

"I'm arranging a ride for you."

"With that?" I reach for the small faux microphone, but the old man is quick. He pulls it away and stashes it between his legs. He explains that it's a special device, that he used to be in the secret service and it's a high-tech gadget that not too many people know about.

I don't care about the gadget or about Yuma; I just want to

186

stay in the comfortable car. I'm like a powerless country with one natural resource, and this man has his eyes on that resource. And because there aren't many cars traveling on the road, and because the radio isn't playing, I start talking to him a little provocatively, coquettishly even, saying for instance that I have nothing against the *idea* of oral sex. And I can see that this excites the man, or distracts him, enough so that he passes the exit, and I think I can keep the man going like this for the next whatever odd miles.

And they are odd. Because the man has a goal, he's persistent, holding his imaginary microphone between his legs, talking occasionally to imaginary agents, listening to me, as the exits go by, as I wonder aloud about blow jobs, trying to walk a line between interested and not *that* interested. But the man is interested and as he's saying it, I'm wondering if his teeth are real.

Gradually, my initial disgust starts to wane. I wouldn't say I'm titillated, but the wall of resistance I had in my mind begins to crumble, partly because it's a perversion of my normal mode, and partly because my normal mode has done nothing for me lately. I'm ready to tell my normal mode to fuck off.

The landscape we're driving through is spotted with cacti and sage and the tentacle stalks of ocotillo rising out of the sand. It's just the four lanes of the highway, two going west, two going east. A few small junkyard shacks pop up now and then, but basically it's flat desert and barren hills. However, at one of the shacks, as we pass, I notice a compact station wagon. Just the one car, and I think that I can see, sitting in the driver's seat, a lone head with the hair of a woman. Not that it matters. It's not Anne's hair, but because the car, which may not even be a station wagon, is more interesting than the horny old man, I tell the driver to let me off.

"Only if we do it," the old man says. He's got both hands

on the steering wheel. I mention the shack and the man says he'll take me there, but "only if we do it."

So, okay. "Fine," I say. And this "fine," when I say it, is the "fine" of surrender. It's not that the man is omnipotent or anything, it's that I'm willing to abdicate my own potency in deference to his. I'm letting him decide what will happen. We don't shake hands, but the man agrees. He drives to the next exit, a crossroads without building or tree, and he pulls off the road and parks the car on an incline overlooking the highway. He puts his plastic microphone back in the glove compartment and tells me to take my "thing" out.

You wouldn't call it coercion because I know I'm not trading my services for anything. I'm pretty certain the man isn't going to drive me back to the junkyard shack, and it doesn't matter. I sit there, staring out the windshield, and the man leans over and does what he does. And it's wetter than I expected, but I try to imagine something, not Anne because Anne is dead, but something like Anne, something to make the event seem a little more normal and comfortable. But as the act continues, I begin to feel slightly *un*comfortable, and then more uncomfortable, and my reaction is to concentrate on something else, on something alive and real. But there's nothing I want to concentrate on.

We're given a life and we have to do something with that life, and at the moment I'm letting the man decide what my life will be doing. And by resting my eyes on the maroon mountains in the distance, and by not looking down at the man's white head in my lap, I am able to imagine that life, and pretend to lead that life, and to bring myself, in not much time, to a climax.

There, I think, that's the bit done.

But not quite. As I zip up my pants I notice that the man is

188

doing something with himself under the steering wheel. And whatever it is it's not working out.

"That was too fast," the man says.

I say something about there being, as far as I could remember, no time stipulation. But the man is unfulfilled and with a raging unfulfilledness he tells me to get out of the car. This doesn't seem completely fair, especially since I've already settled into my seat, but when the man tells me again to get out of the car it seems like probably the easiest solution. So I grab my pack, close the door, and notice, as the man drives away, that he's driving in the direction of Yuma.

As long as I had my need I was able to move forward, but now I've lost what I want, forgotten what I'm doing and where I'm going, and in fact, at the moment, I'm not going anywhere. I've stopped moving. I look down at a desiccated plant beside a gray granite rock and I don't know what I'm thinking, probably not thinking anything, because my body has taken over. My body is feeling like a rock, the heaviness of a rock, except a rock that once wanted something.

The junkyard is out of my mind by now. The heat of the sun is scorching my face, and my shoes, which had always been comfortable shoes, are bothering me. My socks are slipping into my shoes but I don't pull them up. I would stay where I am on the crusted sand but walking is habitual. So I walk down to the overpass, and under the shade of the overpass I wait. Not wait. I'm not waiting for anything. I'm looking at the overpass support columns and behind them to a cool and dirty ledge of cement, and I'm planning a night on that cement.

But the night is a long way away. I wait under that overpass the rest of the day. No food, no drink, not even a mandolin to play. I could take out my notebook and jot down my thoughts, but I don't want to notice my thoughts.

I hardly notice the cars passing by on the highway, and I don't try to recognize a recognizable driver.

There's nothing I can do.

Except walk.

Walking is habitual for me but now I don't even want to walk.

Why walk, I think. Is any spot on the pavement, or any destination, better than any other? No. I actually say the word out loud. "No." And partly I'm saying no to the lack of hope, and partly I'm saying no to hope itself.

It's not that I can't go on, it's just that I don't feel like it.

And you might call this a low point, and I might have called it that, but in calling it that, I would have made it a thing with a name, and since I was a thing with a *different* name, I would have separated myself from the thing I was naming, in this case the quicksand of hopelessness. But I didn't separate myself. Instead I went to the low point, and in a way embraced the low point, and fueled by the feeling I was having, the low point sank even lower.

3

Evening descended on the desert. After a while I found myself in the middle of darkness, literally. Looking up at the night sky beyond the overpass I could see the stars, which would have been considered beautiful, and the moon, having already set— that was also probably beautiful, but I was a thing apart from beauty or the recognition of beauty.

That was when the car pulled over onto the edge of the highway. It was an old brown Mercedes with two guys sitting in the front seat. The passenger window was rolled down and a stubble-faced man was telling me to hop in, hop in, so I did. It was a four-door and I got in the back and off we went.

The passenger was a big guy with stringy, dirty-blond hair. He swung his arm over the seat and said, "Where are you going?"

"Where are *you* going?" I asked him.

And he answered, "All the way, man, just like you."

His name was Jimbo, and the driver, with dark hair, was Craig. They were both drinking from cans of beer, smoking cigarettes, and they seemed extremely friendly. They asked if I could contribute to the gas fund, and when I said I couldn't, they didn't seem to mind. Jimbo passed me a beer and it seemed as if we were all good buddies.

Since they didn't have gas money either, what they would do is pull into gas stations, and Jimbo would go into the store, begin to seem to buy a few bits of food, and then, when Craig had filled the car with gas, Jimbo would run back to the car and they'd drive off without paying. "Living off the land," Craig said. He took the role of the level-headed, intelligent one. Jimbo was wilder and prone to small but detectable fits of anger.

But they seemed to like me, and they convinced me, after a barrage of pointed questions, to tell the story of Anne, which I did, and when I did they told me not to worry. "We'll catch her, man," they said, as if they hadn't heard that she was dead. Although we'd been driving fast enough before that, we drove even faster, as if we might possibly catch up with her.

And I didn't mind.

At a certain point I offered to buy them some real food. I'll pay with my credit card, I thought, and so we stopped at a roadside café near a place called Calexico, sat at a booth by the window, and had some eggs and coffee.

A rotund waitress set paper place mats in front of us, with drawings of desert flora and fauna. Craig and Jimbo ordered a lot of food and they advised me to do the same. "Might be your last supper, man," Craig said.

I nodded without quite knowing why. The waitress wrote the orders on a pad. When Craig said to her, with a lewd smile, "I bet your eggs are the best in town," she tried to smile back. The food came, we ate, I presented my credit card, and when the waitress returned she had bad news. The card wasn't responding. I gave her another and then another and they all turned out to be invalid.

"You're maxed out, man," Craig told me, not upset about it. In fact he went ahead and ordered a pie, to go.

I said something about washing dishes to pay the bill, and Craig said, "Maybe we won't have to." His smile was full of yellow teeth.

"We have to do something," I said. "Wash dishes or . . ."

"Like in a movie, right?" Jimbo said.

And when the pie arrived, all boxed up and tied, Craig announced that he was getting money from the car, and he got up and left. And when the waitress went into the back part of the café, Jimbo got up. I reminded him that we hadn't paid the bill but he kept walking, past the cash register, out the glass door. First Craig, then Jimbo, and I was like a prisoner. I felt like one, and so I surrendered. I unbuckled my watch strap, left my watch on the table, and then I walked out to the car.

They wanted me to enter their world, to join their club, the club of not doing good, and for no reason other than the reason of least resistance I resigned myself to membership of that club, and to whatever and wherever that resignation led. They supplied food and drink and travel, and although I didn't like the idea of stealing everything, I didn't see any alternative except getting out of the car, and since I was in the car I didn't want to get out. And they didn't want me out. They wanted me to be one of them.

"You're staying with us, man. The three amigos."

The beer Jimbo drank was barely cool, the ice they'd once had in their Styrofoam bucket had long ago melted, but they wanted me to drink. It was implied in their encouragement. They were almost demanding that I keep drinking beer. When I asked them to stop at the next bathroom they insisted I pee out the window. I didn't want to pee out the window but I was too tired or too weak, or more likely, I couldn't see what difference it would make. So I knelt on the seat, leaned out as far as I could, and of course I peed all over myself. And the funny thing was, I didn't seem to care. I sat back down in the leather seat and they told me I needed to rest. "You need your energy, man, if you want to find your girlfriend."

"Wife," I told them.

"Whatever," Jimbo said, and he told me to stretch out and relax. And because I was exhausted, I put my head on my backpack. But Craig and Jimbo didn't stop talking, and they didn't stop trying to get me to drink. They seemed to have an endless supply of both words and lukewarm beer, and try as I might to keep up with their drinking, at a certain point I got full of beer, didn't want any beer, and I told them, "I don't want any more."

It wasn't just the beer. It was my unwillingness to listen to them, the sense of being polluted by their words and their attitudes. And at this point the mood might have turned sour except that we were coming down out of the hills, the last range of rocky hills before the coast. And by the time we entered the area of greater metropolitan San Diego the two of them were happy again. They started talking about Anne, as if she wasn't dead, coming up with schemes to find her. "Put an ad in the paper," they said, or "Put up flyers on telephone poles." They knew San Diego like the backs of their dicks, they said, and they told me to relax, to do nothing, and let them take care of everything.

The brown land was frosted with springtime green, but mainly it was covered with houses. Millions of people lived in the subdivisions cut into the hillsides. We drove through a town called El Cajon, which means "the box," and through La Mesa, which means "the table," and I didn't know where we were going, or where I was gong with them, until, following the freeway to the end, we arrived at the Pacific Ocean. Craig parked the car near a pier in a place called Pacific Beach. A lot of people in bathing suits were walking on the streets and it was warm, even before summer.

Craig and Jimbo told me to watch the car while they got out, walked across a nearby intersection, and returned with bags full of hamburgers and french fries. They divvied up the waxy paper bags and as we were about to eat Craig realized we didn't have any ketchup. "Can't eat without ketchup," he said, and I was the one volunteered to go back to the fast-food restaurant and get some.

Which I did. It felt good to stretch my legs and see people again. No one looked up when I walked to the condiment counter and grabbed a large handful of ketchup packages. I took this booty back to the waiting car, but the car wasn't waiting. I looked in various parking lots, and it wasn't there. It wasn't parked on the street, and it wasn't circling the street, and although I waited for them, pacing back and forth, hoping they went to get some gas, I knew that now, here I was, with nothing. I threw the ketchup packages into a plastic trash container.

I didn't mind losing my pack or my clothes or even my notebook. But my photographs were in that pack. Anne, or what was left of Anne, was in that car. There was still a memory, the trace of memory, but everything else was gone. And I tried to see this as something new, a fresh start. I told myself that now, with nothing, I was a new man. I tried to see myself as reborn, but by this point I was getting a little tired of being constantly reborn.

4

I was thinking about Chief Joseph, the leader of the Nez Perce
Indians, who in 1877 was put on a reservation. He had signed
a treaty with the United States government, but because of a
gold rush on his ancestral land was forced to flee that land and
fight for that land, until, when the hopelessness of his struggle
became obvious, he surrendered. "I am tired," he said. "I will
fight no more forever." He was then taken to a reservation where
he survived to see his people decimated by disease.

He didn't have to survive, I thought. And I didn't have to
survive, but it was habit now, or genetic, and once I got my
bearings, the first thing I did was make a phone call. I was
going to call and get some money, but to make a call I needed
money, and I didn't have any, not even a thin quarter, so I stood
by the entrance to a convenience store near the beach and asked
people coming out for change.

Simple enough, I thought. I was an honest-looking person,
and as people walked out of the Speedy Mart or the Quick Mart
I tried to explain my situation. "What happened to me . . ." but
before I could get started the people left me standing in the
gum-stained entrance. So I changed my approach, got straight
to the point. "Can I have a quarter?" I said, first to a woman,
then to a girl, then a man, and you'd think, by the way these
people refused to look at me, that a quarter was a lot of money.

For a while no one even acknowledged my existence, so
instead of asking them to put a quarter in my open palm, I

found a plastic bag and held that out, and maybe it was the bag or a new attitude, anyway, someone finally put a quarter in the bag and with it I called American Express.

I was thinking they would help, but after finally getting through to the woman on the other end, she told me that my card had been terminated. I asked if it was possible to get a loan and I could tell by her tone of voice, even over the phone, even though she was calling me "sir," that I didn't really exist for her. She didn't say anything disrespectful—the call might have been monitored—but I got the idea I was on my own.

Fine, I thought. Or as Jimbo used to say, Whatever.

Since I was close to the water I walked down to the white cement boardwalk, to a wooden pier, called Crystal Pier, jutting into the ocean. I walked out to the end of it, and I could see in one direction the sun reflected into broken shards of light on the water, and in the other direction, the land and the city and the mountains in the distance. I walked from there to the beach itself, across the sand, and although I didn't have a bathing suit, I found a less populated spot, secluded by eroding cliffs; stripped down to my underwear; and waded out into the waves.

The water was colder than I expected but I was a man of adjustment, and so I got used to that. When I was far enough out, I dove in and swam, playing in the waves, holding my underwear to keep it from slipping off. In the water I felt some-what rejuvenated, and I stayed there until my fingers started to wrinkle. Back on the beach, I stood in the sun, letting it warm me and letting my underwear dry.

Although I never got one of those hamburgers, my hunger wasn't terrible, and with my clothes back on I walked to what they called the boardwalk. There weren't any actual boards, but there was a cement wall separating the littoral world from the civilized world and I sat on that. Looking off into the blue water, I could hear the sound of skateboard wheels, the conversations of freckled couples, and the cries of scavenger seagulls circling over my head.

That's when I heard someone calling out, "Van Belle!"

I heard the words but they had no meaning for me.

"Van Belle?"

And yet for some reason I thought the calling was aimed at me, as if some person recognized me, and so without assuming I was the target of the calling, I turned. A scrabbly man crouched against the cement wall was calling me over.

"Remember me?" he said, and he sat up and smiled as if smiling for a photo. "Steve Polino," he said. "From Claremont. You're Van Belle, right?"

I nodded, thinking I might as well go along with it.

This Polino fellow asked me if I was hungry. "I know all about bad times," he said, and he took me to a dumpster behind a taco stand, one of several he said he knew about, and we found, down in the bowels of the dumpster, some leftover Mexican food wrapped in clear plastic bags. The food inside was just a lot of rice with bean juice in Styrofoam containers, no tamales or enchiladas, but we scraped off the specks of dirt and pieces of congealed lard, and with some containers of salsa we sat together on a bus-stop bench, enjoying our starchy repast.

This was the beginning of living on the beach. Polino took me under his wing, showing me where to find food and where to clean up. He took me to his shelter and invited me to stay. It was near the beach, in a maintenance room in the Surfer Hotel, a cinder-block room with a drain in the concrete floor, and most of it was taken up with the hotel's heating and cooling system. Which meant it was warm at night and there was a comforting white-noise drone in the background. Somehow Polino had a key, so it was private, our cavelike home, and all we had to do was make sure we cleared out during the day.

I call it a home because Polino had it set up with some domestic touches. Behind the heating unit he'd hidden a box with books and blankets, and he gave me a blanket, or loaned it, and sometimes, on cold days, we wrapped ourselves in our blankets and sat on the beach in the fog, contemplating the enveloping grayness. We lived the beachcomber life together, or in close proximity of each other. Our gainful employment was panhandling, but our main activity was sitting on the cement wall separating the beach from the boardwalk and developing our tans. Polino was already deeply bronzed, with an added layer of dirt that protected him from the sun. It's called a home-less tan, and sitting outside all day, day after day, I began, inad-vertently, to develop my own.

Bums, or people called bums, are largely invisible. People with regular lives don't like to see people living on the street so they don't. But in the cracks and corners of the world these people also have to eat. As did I. Which meant I had to beg on the street or scrounge in the trash, and the problem was, I didn't like it. I could have adjusted, but because I saw it as a tempo-rary state, I didn't. I didn't submit to my new lifestyle, and told Polino that I wasn't going to live like this for long.

"What's the matter with living like this?"

"It's not the way to live," I told him. But it happened to be Polino's way to live, so he was slightly insulted.

"How do you want to live?" he said.

"Not like this," I said.

"You have something better?"

"I don't intend to keep eating out of dumpsters," I said. I told him I planned on getting a job.

Anne always wanted me to get a job, or a better job. I remem-bered—I wasn't sure it was Anne—a girl walking barefoot on some hot asphalt somewhere, telling me to be ambitious. Was it Anne? It probably was Anne but why was I always thinking about Anne? Anne was dead. I wasn't dead. I was determined to remember other things, new things. I wanted to remember new things, but the problem was, I didn't. Days went by and I didn't do anything but sleep and eat and sit on the boardwalk wall with Polino. I could have remembered that, but it wasn't very memorable.

I'd given up the idea of calling my friends. I realized that I didn't have any friends. All my friends were Anne's friends. New York was part of another life. The memory of it lingered, a little, and one time, walking across the warm sand, I told Polino about my life with Anne.

But he was unsympathetic. "She's gone, dude. Get over it."

"Fine," I said. "Whatever." And even though I said "Whatever," and even though I continued eating out of dumpsters, I refused, in my mind, to become part of Polino's world. It was a pathetic world, I thought. Not my world, and yet all the time I thought I was resisting that world and the indolence of that world, I was succumbing. I needed to survive and that's what I did.

I had a job, briefly. Polino, it turned out, never bothered to learn how to drive, and when a friend offered him a job driving someone in a car, I took it. I was to drive a girl—in her car—to a house. She was to go inside and I was to wait in the car and, in case of emergency, to come into the house, which I was assured would never be necessary. When the night of my job arrived I walked to the girl's house. She was waiting for me, all business. "You don't look too good," she said, and although she told me I smelled bad, she let me drive her to the house where she had a massage appointment. She went into the house while I listened to the radio and watched the quiet residential street and the light from the streetlight shining on a nearby garden. When she came out of the house, about an hour later, she started yelling at me. She told me I was fired. "You're too dirty," she said. "It's bad for my reputation." I didn't know what had happened. I would've argued my case, but I didn't really care about my case. Why should I care? When she reached into her purse I told her to keep her money, which seemed to mollify her, and then I drove her home. I walked through the nighttime streets back to my makeshift shelter where I curled up with my blanket and listened to the humming of the air-conditioning machines.

Living on the edge of the continent, at the edge of society, I was feeling less and less connected to the world. I was pretty sure the massage girl had spoken to me, but whatever had happened between us, I was obviously of little consequence. I was more or less invisible. And when I say I didn't care, it wasn't specifically the incident with the girl. I cared about nothing. Or almost nothing. There was *one* thing, one small ember of desire still burning in me. Given a chance, I would have said that I wanted to be loved. But given the growing inconsequentiality of my life, and the fact that the girl hadn't even recognized me as a living being, I was lowering my sights. I wanted to be loved, yes, but at this point it was enough to simply exist. It's fine, I said to myself, and if it wasn't completely fine, or perfectly fine, at least it was somewhat bearable.

Gradually I submitted to the way of Polino, the way of doing the least amount of anything. As I got used to eating garbage I let my disgust fade away, and it was liberating to do this. To surrender to the least resistance. That's what I thought I was doing. Not fighting the world, or society, or the events of my life, but forgetting them. That's what I thought.

5

One day Polino and I were walking down an alley off the main Mission Beach boulevard. We were talking about some girl Polino had seen, watching the people walk to the beach, and Polino told me he'd been married, so it surprised me when he then said, "Look, here come our dates." I looked up as two girls were crossing the street in our direction. And just about as I saw them I felt this object hit me in the stomach. It was an avocado. A partially eaten avocado rolled onto the sidewalk and I looked up and saw a man running down the alley. Another man staggered up to us and said that his friend was drinking too much and didn't know what he was doing. Well fine, I thought, okay, no problem. A drunk, right? What are you going to do?

I scraped the green mush off my shirt, looked up, and of course by then the girls had gone. I was standing there, talking with Polino, and I heard this *"Hijo de puta."* I turned around and the avocado man was back. He was standing by a telephone pole saying, *"Hijo de puta."* To me. *"Hijo de puta, hijo de puta,"* making an obscene gesture at me with his hand.

Okay. The man was drunk. So okay, we tried ignoring him. We tried to carry on a conversation, but *"Hijo de puta, hijo de puta,"* he kept saying it, and I didn't know what it meant but this constant *"Hijo de puta, hijo de puta,"* whatever it was, was beginning to get to me. I thought I probably knew, more or less, what was right and what was wrong and what the man was doing wasn't right.

"Hijo de puta, hijo de puta." The man didn't stop, he just kept pounding away and finally it snapped, or I snapped, and I took a few steps toward the man, to chase him away or teach him a lesson. Sometimes you have to use might in the service of justice, sometimes you just have to *do* something. I was thinking this as the man ran up the street.

Okay. Fine. Except the man came back. And he kept saying, over and over, *"Hijo de puta, hijo de puta."* And I was going to chase him again but instead of that I thought, I can say it too, and I did. *"Hijo de puta."*

And the man said it back. *"Hijo de puta."*

I said it, and the man said it, *Hijo de puta. Hijo de puta,* back and forth, and the man was holding a flashlight, shining it toward me in the broad daylight, and even though it was having no effect, I wanted my own flashlight, to shine at him.

And right about at that moment I realized that I could have stepped back. I could have stepped away and seen the situation clearly. I could have stepped away from myself and just quit, just let go. I could have done that, but I didn't. I felt that I was *in* this thing, that I was part of this *hijo de puta, hijo de puta* . . .

Desire is hard to get rid of. Even twisted desire, or especially twisted desire, like a weed, keeps coming up. By this time a crowd had gathered along the sides of the alley and a fat guy with a flag decal on his jacket back was urging me to "make the sucker eat shit." And I was inclined to agree. They weren't inciting me, but there I was, and there was this person, and somehow I felt trapped in the structure of this relationship we were creating.

That's when I noticed, out of the corner of my eye, another man, a short man, standing by a redwood fence. He was saying, *"Mira, mira,"* and I didn't see what he was referring to, or even think there was anything there to see. I'd seen everything I wanted to see, but the short man kept looking at me, and I thought he was talking to me, so I turned and looked around, and there was no way to know what he was trying to indicate, but what I saw when I looked made it all not matter. Walking up the street I saw the British guy from Kentucky.

It took a while for me to make the connection, a few seconds, and it might have been the beginning of hope, but I thought I'd had enough of hope. There was always hope and then inevitably the dissolution of that hope, and now I was just about done with hope. Except not quite.

I saw the man named Geoff, wearing a blue Hawaiian shirt, coming out of a sushi restaurant and walking alone up the street. I left Polino and the flashlight man, and followed Geoff, from a distance, following him around a corner and along a neatly manicured residential street named after a semiprecious stone. He crossed a street, walked into the next block, and went into one of the houses. I didn't see which house exactly, but there were only a finite number of houses on the block and I imagined I'd know it when I came to it. And when I did come to it, there it was, sitting in the morning fog, a one-story bungalow with the two familiar cars parked, one in the driveway and one on the street.

I didn't think of Anne because Anne was gone. I was thinking of the girl who wasn't Anne.

My favorite expression during my time with Polino was "Fuck it." When something presented itself I would just, with my newfound habit, say Fuck it. Meaning just treat everything as something not to care about. To want nothing else. To hate who I was. Fuck my body and my hair and my teeth, and also my desires. Especially fuck them. But now they were fucking me. I could feel them coming to life in my body, and I mentioned before about how desire turns into hope which turns into anticipation, and for me, anticipation had become a force, like a thing at the end of a rope, pulling, and I could feel myself being pulled, through the membrane that separated me from hope, pulling me out of Polino's world and into something else.

That something else was the view of Linda's house.

I walked past the house several times on the sidewalk, like a pedestrian, casually sneaking looks in the curtained window. I stood across the street, under the weeping branches of a willow tree, silently watching, like an Indian, for her to emerge. And waiting. And as I waited I imagined her, which kept me waiting. When she appeared, watering the terracotta pots on the front steps, I felt in my body a longing. Not necessarily for her but for something that I wanted. I wanted it with the excruciating want of a child wanting, and what was excruciating was my belief in the impossibility of even getting near it. It was in my heart, this thing that I wanted so much, and what was in my heart was love.

There was the fact that I loved Anne. Which I still did. And she loved me. She had and she did. Love had definitely existed, and I was happy in that love. I was happy to love, and also happy to *be* loved by her. Although she was gone, my need or my habit or my desire for her still existed.

And you might say, "That's over." You might say, "Move on and find someone else to love." And that would be the correct prescription. Get on with your life, Jack. And it's easy to say that, but for me it wasn't so easy. I didn't want to move on. I didn't want to replace my love. And anyway, I didn't see how I could. Where would the old love go? Into memory? I had plenty of memories already. I didn't need more memories. I needed Anne. I loved her and she's dead and I know she's dead but I can't just turn around, see someone new, and love that new person. And yes, I might like to be loved again, who wouldn't? But I want Anne's love. That's the love I got used to, and having got used to it, I want it back.

Standing there, watching Linda, I start to imagine, in my mind, not a perfect person, because I don't need perfection anymore. I'm not perfect, but I want a person to give my love to. As if something inside me needs to leave my body and find an object outside my body. As I stare at the purple bougainvillea vine blooming over the door, more than seeing any one specific person, I imagine a generalized person, a woman. I conceive of a love for her. I imagine her imperfections and it's those imperfections that I see myself loving. And she, in my dreams, is willing to return my love. My fantasies, as I run them through my mind, over and over, become, not quite reality, but something I can live for.

6

I'm excited about the prospect of . . . what? I don't know exactly, excited more by the emergence of desire than the possibility of that desire getting rewarded. I go back to the bunker where I live, find Polino spreading out his blanket, and because Polino is, at the moment, my best friend, I share my excitement.

I tell him about Linda, and about Geoff and Kentucky, but Polino has already heard about Anne, and this new girl, whoever she is, means nothing to him. He changes the subject, starts discoursing to me about the Donner Party, the people who crossed the Sierra Nevada, or tried to, but bad planning or unexpected weather forced them to stay the winter and starve. Or, if not starve, to eat their fellow travelers. He's going on about the winter of 1847 and partly I'm listening to the lecture and partly I'm thinking about the lecturer.

Polino is wiry and energetic, and it's not that he doesn't have ambition. I've noticed that in his choice of words, although there are the requisite catch phrases of the day, he also likes to experiment with words he doesn't know, or wants to know. The two books in his box are a ragged copy of *Hamlet* and a badly torn dictionary. Really half a dictionary—only the letters M through Z—and in the middle of his explanation of old-time cannibalism, as he describes the state of mind of the hungry families, he uses the word "lachrymosity." And he stops in the middle of his speech. He's not sure the word exists, and of course in his tattered dictionary the word isn't there, and the fact that the definition of the word, if it is a word, is unknown to him increases his belief that knowing its meaning would change things.

So he's frustrated, and in his frustration looks around and sees me, sitting against the cinder-block wall, and he suddenly says to me, "This is my house, you know."

"I know," I say. "I appreciate your hospitality."

"Hospitality?"

I can see what he wants is a little recognition. Although he's living a life of indolence he still has some flickering desire. He too wants to be seen, and although he's not willing to admit it, or do anything to bring it about, he's tired of the free and easy life of romance, which for him lacks any actual romance.

I'm not blind to his dissatisfaction. Although it's directed at me, I see it as stemming from something else, and I believe I can change that dissatisfaction. I'm feeling the anticipation of making contact with Linda and I want to pass on that feeling of anticipation. Having found a way out of my own tar pit, I want to pull Polino out. So I come up with a plan.

And the first thing I need to implement this plan is a goal. Sex is a good one, I think, so first comes the pep talk, a motivational sermon to get Polino going. I begin coaxing Polino into describing the girl he's been talking about, a blond beachcomber girl he's seen strolling along the beach. The thought of this girl gets him over his resistance.

That's the first step.

The second step is getting cleaned up.

I take off my pants and shirt, get Polino to do the same, and then, in my underwear, I wash the clothes in a public shower by the beach. Using some soap that had fallen into the drain, I scrub and rinse and wash, first our clothes, then my body and my hair and my face. Polino leaves his beard alone, but with an abandoned disposable razor, I cut the incipient stubble off my face.

Wearing only our underwear, we set our clothes out on the rim of a trash can to dry. People are watching us but we don't care, and partially we don't care, or at least I don't care, because I feel different now that I'm clean, or cleaner, and I believe Polino feels the same.

Grudgingly, he admits that he does. He begins to engage himself with the world of possibility, and the next step would be a haircut, but because I can't find any scissors or comb we brush our hair back with our fingers.

And then comes finding the girl. Which would be simple enough except that Polino, having lived so long as a hermit, has lost his confidence. He's lost belief in himself, in his own likability. But we've come this far, together, and so with our clothes dried, our hair combed, we go out into the world. We stand in front of a bar on Garnet Avenue and what we need, or what Polino says he needs, is a beer. But for that we need more money, so instead we buy a can of beer from a store and take up our position near the lifeguard station.

We see a girl in bikini and sandals, but she's not the right girl. Polino has very defined criteria for the person he's willing to share his beer with and so we stroll around, past people in restaurants watching waves, past surfer-themed bars, and motels with lawns like putting greens.

And then we find her. She's not blond, but that's okay. She's sitting on the public grass in cut-off jeans, braiding her hair, and when we sit with her she doesn't walk away. A conversation is started and we learn she's from out of town. She's got long black hair and Polino offers her his beer. I can see that all my motivational talk was nothing compared to a real living person, wearing a shirt several sizes too small, looking at Polino and listening to him, and seeming to be interested. Gradually I extricate myself, leaving Polino alone with the girl, talking and braiding and feeling the worm of desire.

I go back to Linda's house.

I stand across the street in the shelter of the same weeping willow, and from the protection of this vantage I start my vigil. Her car is still parked on the street so I wait. After about an hour and a half, when she finally does walk out of the front door, I'm not sure what I'm going to say. I've rehearsed it a thousand times but now when I'm confronted with the real object, slightly different and less malleable than the fantasy object, I begin to waver.

Linda walks to the driver's side of the maroon station wagon, takes her keys out of her pants—sweatpants that conform to the contour of her legs—and that's when desire, the enemy of sloth, sets me in motion. I start running. I've waited so long that now, before she gets in the car and drives away, I have to run to her. She looks up, sees this man running toward her, but she isn't scared. By the time I get to her and stop in front of her, I'm breathing more than I would like.

"Remember me?" I say.

Of course she does.

"I've moved to San Diego."

"That's a coincidence," she says.

She's wearing a T-shirt.

"Are you a surfer?" she says.

"A body surfer?"

"You've got a tan like a surfer."

"From the sun," I say. "How are you? Are you off to work?"

"To a class," she says.

"A class in what? What subject?"

She just looks at me. Although the question never gets

officially answered we find ourselves talking about the Scripps aquarium and Torrey Pines park and how the actual Torrey pine tree is structurally more like a fir than a pine tree. Our conversation bounces around but she seems to enjoy my somewhat overzealous attention. We talk for a while, standing at the side of her car, and then she says, "Would you like to get together, later?"

I nod, tell her that I would, and so we arrange to meet. The idea of a picnic is mentioned. I watch her get into the station wagon and drive off, and as I walk away, I'm feeling as close to happiness as I can remember feeling in a long time.

7

That afternoon, back at the boardwalk, I find Polino, shirt-less, sitting against the boardwalk wall, looking out toward the ocean and the clouds above the ocean, holding in his hand a brown paper bag with a beer inside. He doesn't offer me any when I sit beside him, and I can see that, although I'm happy, Polino is not so happy. It turns out that the girl on the grass had no interest in him, that he got his hopes up for nothing, that he'd promised himself he would never get his hopes up because bad things always happen and now he did and they did and he's pissed off. At me. "You set me up, man."

I can see, or think I can see, behind the anger, to Polino's sadness. And I sympathize. I feel a fondness for this person, but when I ask what happened, all he wants to tell me is that he fell on his face. "I fell, man. I forgot what it feels like but now I remember. The oldest rule in the book."

I don't ask him which book he's referring to, and he goes on about what an asshole he is and how stupid he is, and I mention something Shakespearean about assuming a trait if you lack it.

"Fuck that," he says.

"It's from Shakespeare," I say.

"I know what it is, fuckhead." And then he launches into a disputation on the nonexistence of Shakespeare. "He's a fake, man. He didn't exist."

"As a writer, you mean?"

"Believe any half-assed bullshit you want, man, if it floats your fucking canoe."

"Are you saying he's dead?" I ask, and we don't exactly argue about Shakespeare because I don't know the whole history of Shakespearean scholarship on the subject, but I think Shakespeare probably existed. And even if he didn't, I would like to believe, and find it useful to believe, that he did.

But Polino's not going along with that. "I don't believe in anything," he says, "unless it's in front of my face." He pulls out a cigarette from behind his ear, tears off the filter, and with it, gestures across the beach. "I believe *this*. This is my life," he says, "and I like it."

That's what he says, but really I think he dreams of a different life. And the problem is desire. He wishes that something would change, but he's made a calculation, at some level, that it's easier to deny his desires than to have them. He knows desire won't ever get him anything but more desire and so he's short-circuited the chain of desire, thinking that now he doesn't have it, that he's free and unencumbered, and he makes a case for his own happiness because of that supposed freedom.

But like the sea behind a seawall, the desire is still there. His finger in the dike has gotten used to holding it back—it's a habit—and so it doesn't seem unusual. He's convinced himself that he wants nothing and needs nothing, and to keep this myth alive he won't allow himself to feel the dissatisfaction pounding against the wall in front of him. He believes in the myth of the carefree life of no desire, which, although it's called carefree, actually takes a lot of work.

He drops his cigarette into the beer can, throws it toward a trash bin, and it lands, because of the wind, in the sand. This little four-second movie, as I replay it to myself, brings up a

213

memory of Anne—I think it was Anne—dropping a beer can into a stream in the Catskill Mountains.

We were walking along a rocky streambed near a friend's house. Other people were with us and we were all drinking beer, and when she finished her beer, instead of holding on to it, she looked for a place to leave her can where it wouldn't be so obvious. She knew that what she was doing was wrong, and the fact that she knew it made it worse. At the time I tried to love her and overlook this—not indiscretion, but this thoughtless and ugly act. Although she wasn't ugly, it made her seem ugly, and I begin to remember that she wasn't completely beautiful, not unadorned beauty, and that my love for her had lapses. For a long time I was able to overlook those lapses, and was happy overlooking them.

Now I say something to Polino about leaving trash on the beach, and Polino tells me he's tired of my goddamn goody-goodness. "Don't walk around here if you don't like it," he says. "Walk someplace else."

Being the conciliator, I say something like "Yeah" or "Whatever."

But Polino has renounced, not only his desires, but me, who, strangely enough, represents desire, and when he tells me to leave, to fuck off and get out, what he's really saying is, Don't destroy my world.

So fine, I think, and I tell Polino that I'll see him later.

He says, "You don't get it, Van Belle. I don't want to see you later. I want to see you never. Go to a different beach. Find some other beach to do your . . . This is my beach."

So I apologize. "I didn't mean to . . ."

"Go fuck yourself," he says.

I stand there, not moving.

"Fuck you," he says, and he walks away.

And then I walk away.

And ever the man to adust, I adjust to this. Okay, I think, and I walk to another beach. I have my meeting with Linda, and this meeting has become, or Linda has become, not the light at the end of a tunnel because I'm not in a tunnel, but a beacon, let's say, or a lighthouse.

I take a swim that afternoon. In my underwear I swim out far enough so that I'm floating in the salt water, beyond where the waves are breaking, away enough from everything I know to feel free of everything I know. I can feel the water surrounding my skin, the buoyancy of the water, the swells of water cradling me. I imagine what it might be like, taking a last breath and going down, under the water, holding my breath until I can't hold it anymore and then, when the time comes, when the breath runs out, to let the water come into me and take me. That would be fine. It would almost be desirable, except there's the human urge to maintain buoyancy. I can feel the water pushing me, incessantly, back to the shore, back to the world. And after a while I'm ready to go back. I'm ready to go back, and yet at the same time, I feel that I could float on the water forever.

VII

Avaritia

1

Although the idea of sin is almost extinct, there are still certain things, certain habits of mind around which human beings seem to orbit. By habits of mind I mean the distractions that fill our world, the things we hate and love and get used to. We don't want to let them go. I don't want to let them go. I'm standing at the La Jolla Cove, in San Diego, orbiting now around something, and whatever it is, I can feel it pulling me. I'm looking out over the green lawn with the cypress trees and palm trees, and there's Linda, spreading a blanket on the grass. She's sitting on her knees, pulling out picnic items from a wicker basket.

It's sunny and cool and I sit beside her on the worn wool blanket. I'm looking forward to talking with her, to sharing with her something profound and personal. I'm searching, down in what I call my gut, for something with which to begin our conversation, and it's not that I'm empty, but before I can find anything down there, or even find the place where something might be hidden, she asks me a simple, unprofound question about living on the beach.

"Living?" I say.

"Isn't that what you do?"

"Well, yes," I say.

"I don't see how you manage," she says.

I shrug. I don't know what to say. There's nothing in me that I can think of. I'm relying on her to do the talking.

"It's a beautiful day today," she says.

We both look out to the sea. And as we do, I can sense her go into herself, into her private thoughts, which is where I would like to go, into *her* life and *her* personality, to reach across the space between us and find—not love, but there's something I want from her, a feeling I want to have, and if I could get it, then love wouldn't matter.

"I hope it lasts," she says.

"Me too," I say.

My interest in her is obvious. She can see that I like her, and although she likes that, because she doesn't want to lead me on, she begins talking about seagulls. She says they make her nervous. She tells me about an arch that used to exist, carved by the sea in the sandstone cliffs, and that over time, because of the sea's incessant pounding, the bridge of the arch has worn away, and the thing that used to be there, that you used to be able to walk across, is gone.

When I don't respond about the rocks, she begins busying herself with the picnic basket. She's brought olives and napkins and sandwiches, and she begins unpacking and organizing these things on the green blanket. The seagulls are flying overhead, gliding against the breeze off the water, and one seagull drops a load of shit. It lands in the grass at the edge of the blanket and she doesn't like it. She stands up to move the blanket, but I have an idea. "An idea," I say, and I walk over to a wooden building at the edge of the grass. It's a bridge club for senior citizens and some broad-leafed plants are growing near this building. I find a large flat leaf from the bottom of a bush and I pull it off the stalk. I go to the turd and attempt to scoop the turd up in the leaf. But because it's not a solid piece of turd, it doesn't want to be scooped up. "Come on," I say. I'm talking to the little gray guano. "Come on into the leaf." And it's easier, in a way, talking to a turd than a human being. And because it's also slightly ridiculous, Linda begins smiling. And smiling is good, so I keep trying, unsuccessfully, to scoop it up. She's still smiling when we finally decide to move the blanket, and when we do, and as her smiling dies down, I start wondering, Why couldn't I be with her? Why couldn't *that* be my life? We seem to get along, and I'm energized by this sense of getting along and the potential for future getting along. When she pulls at the bottom of her shirt I tell her that I understand how someone might want that.

She holds up the arm of her yellow shirt. "It wicks moisture away from the body," she says.

"Your shirt," I say.

"Supposedly."

She's talking about her shirt.

"What do you mean?" she says.

"I mean that it must not be made of cotton," I say.

And although our conversation is not in absolute sync, it doesn't matter, because in my proximity to her I feel that I exist. I believe the casual touching, as we reach for sandwiches, and her acknowledgment of that touching, means that the world we're creating is real. I'm enjoying the sense of reality, thinking about how I can maintain my promixity to that reality when she begins unwrapping her sandwich. My sandwich is still in its plastic on the blanket, but she unwraps hers. She begins eating hers. Not just eating; she brings her whole attention to the act of eating, absorbing herself in the fact of eating, staring at nothing as she chews each bite of basil leaf and mozzarella and the red tomato between the slices of bread.

I'm sitting cross-legged on the blanket, my knee almost touching her knee, but like a tree in the proverbial forest, I seem, for a moment, not to exist.

And then she finishes eating. She looks up.

"There you are," she says, blinking her eyes. "Are you ready?"

She doesn't focus immediately, but when she does she sees me, and we begin packing up the picnic supplies. You'd be able to see in my eyes that I want to stay with her or walk with her, to somehow be with her, and I'm disappointed that what I want doesn't happen. She has to meet Geoffrey, she says. She's in love with Geoffrey.

And because I'm disappointed, and because I'm letting that disappointment show, and because she doesn't want to be the cause of my disappointment, she invites me to dinner.

"Tonight?" I say.

"If you want," she says.

And I say that yes, I can make it. I have no previous engagements. I tell her I'd be happy to come, and I want her to see that I know it's just a dinner, nothing more, just an invitation, but that's enough. If I could have that, I wouldn't need anything more.

2

I spend the rest of the afternoon wandering along Garnet Avenue, aimlessly watching the quotidian world of people driving cars, walking dogs, stepping out of dental offices. In an effort to merge with that world I walk up to a gray-haired woman and ask her for directions to the nearest supermarket. Even though I already know where the supermarket is, I'm grateful to the woman for talking to me. I can tell she's happy to talk, pleased to be practicing the ritual of talking, glad to be useful or real. And for a few minutes I feel real. But I can also feel myself fading, feel that the woman, even before she ends her speech, has forgotten I'm there, that even before she turns and walks away, the brief reality we'd created is gone.

I try it again, this time with a man, his hair tied back in a ponytail. He walks up a street with vines growing over the sidewalk and I follow him to the corner. While he's waiting for the light to change I get close to him and look at him and I would speak to him but so many other things are going on. A million things are happening—the cars and the houses and the weeds in the cracks in the sidewalk. When I don't pay attention to any one of them, in that moment of not paying attention, they seem not to exist. For a moment the man has left my mind, and when I turn back to him he's already crossing the street. He's already walking away, getting smaller and smaller and smaller.

I'm trying to fill the time of waiting with something other than waiting, but all I do is wait. I notice, while I'm waiting, the obvious fact of the sun on my skin or the bus-stop bench I'm sitting on, but my concern isn't the bus-stop bench. My concern is later, the future, and then the future arrives.

I'm sitting at a table with Geoff and Linda, in a crowded Japanese restaurant. I seem to be able to listen, to direct my mind away from the thought of my feet in my shoes, and by listening I seem to be able to keep the world intact. I can hear Geoff talking about picture frames, the existential implications of picture frames. He works at a frame-making shop and he's talking about how a picture frame, by eliminating the extraneous distractions of the world, imposes order on the world. By focusing attention on a limited field of awareness, even an empty frame on a blank wall causes us to see the wall, and the color of the wall, and the cracks in the plaster, in a way we would never have noticed before. He says that without the frame—he's talking about the metaphorical frame—the world would turn into chaos. Which is fine for him, because his frame is solid and firm and agreed upon.

My frame, on the other hand, is fading away, which is why, after Linda serves herself from the various dishes of food, I reach over, take the large spoon, and start scooping food onto my empty plate. I want to try everything, I think. Load it on, I think, and I keep filling my plate until the plate is piled with food. I separate my chopsticks, but when I look down at the pyramid of rice and tofu and green pieces of vegetable, although I would like to have even the slightest desire to eat, I don't. I have the desire for desire, but not desire itself. I can't even imagine taking a bite, or if I did, that eating food is something I'm capable of doing.

I can hear the background sounds of the restaurant; the voices and the clattering, and I look at my bowl of soup. I squirt some sauce from a plastic container into the soup, but it's not the soup that's a problem, it's me, or something lacking in me, and I try to recall the smell of soup and the enjoyment of that smell, and I imagine that maybe there is a certain flavor. I take an experimental slurp, hoping to taste something, but there's nothing to taste except in my imagination. I know it's my imagination, and even my imagination is wavering, like a radio with bad reception. Nothing seems to exist unless I make it exist, so that's what I do.

Which would be fine except that Linda, at this point, is looking at me, waiting for me to say something. And it's not that I have nothing to say, but anything I had has already passed away. Not only that, I feel that *I* am passing away. I want to extricate myself from the sense of this passing and prove that, yes, I exist, but since I can't think of any logical way to do that, I excuse myself and walk to the bathroom.

I close the door and go, not to a urinal, but to a toilet stall. I sit on the toilet, hoping that something might happen to give me a frame of reference, or bring my current frame of reference back to something manageable and real. I try to relax, to let the muscles, if they *are* muscles, do the work they're made for, but nothing seems to be happening. Sitting there, I remember when Anne and I used to be in the bathroom together. It was nothing out of the ordinary but I liked it, and I realize that no one will ever see me sit on a toilet again. No one will ever see the parts of me that matter, never know the person I was when I was most alive. Only Anne would know that and now she's gone.

When I return to the table, Linda and Geoff are still talking to each other, leaning into each other. I can see Geoff's hand, just below the table, probably reaching over to Linda's jean-covered thigh. Their two hands are probably touching, and I can see the love that exists between these two people. I picture them sealed inside a bubble of love, a bubble in which they seem to have found some happiness, a bubble that I will never penetrate. They're in one bubble and I'm in a different bubble, and the bubble I'm in seems to be getting more and more impenetrable. I'm disappearing. I haven't gone away completely, but I'm disappearing, and I won't go without putting up a fight.

When the two of them finish eating, Geoff, who apparently is an amateur photographer, begins taking pictures of Linda. He has a camera with special low-light film, and with it he takes one, then another, and what about me? What about my picture? I strike a pose, waiting for him to turn to me, but he seems interested only in Linda, in taking pictures of Linda, so I ask him, a little aggressively, "Are you a professional photographer?"

"Hardly," he says. "I'm an amateur."

"An amateur?" I say, and for some reason it bothers me that Geoff is the one with the camera. Although it's aimed at other people, notably Linda, the person behind the camera is in charge of framing the event. The camera is recording what's happening, but it's the photographer's eye that places it into memory. And maybe it's memory I want because when Geoff sets the camera on the table I reach out. I say, "May I?" and before he can answer, I'm holding the camera, looking down into the viewfinder. I'm looking down into a mirror reflecting the world, looking at Geoff then Linda, panning back and forth, and it takes me a while to adjust to the—not distortion, but because I'm looking through a mirror that reverses what I'm looking at, what seems to be one side is really the other.

Being a man of adjustment, however, I adjust to this new way of looking. I aim the lens at Linda and press the button that controls the shutter. I take first one picture, then another, shots of Linda and the restaurant and the busboys moving between the tables. And then Geoff. "Hold still," I say, and at first he tries to dodge the camera's lens. "I'd rather you not," he says, but I keep winding and clicking and firing away, shot after shot of Geoff's outstretched hand in front of his face, and after a while the lowering of his hand. I'm not even focusing, just snapping as fast as I can, each individual picture becoming a frame in a movie that somehow might capture him. Or capture the world.

My connection with the world is dying, and naturally, it's something I want to maintain. When I sight Geoff in the camera I'm not trying to kill him. I'm not married to Linda. I'm just trying to save my place in the world. Even when the film runs out I keep snapping and snapping, in a frenzy of photographic greed that leaves me, when I finally stop snapping, as unconnected as I was before.

I put the camera back on the table.

"Anytime you want to use it," Geoff says.

And the way he says it, and the way he looks at me when he says it, makes me think that, not only does he mean it, but that in letting me go a little crazy, he was accepting me as a living person.

He seems to be asking if I can be trusted, telling me, with his eyes, that *he* can be trusted. And trust is good, and I look at him and try to signal that I also think it's good. I can see the generosity in his attempt to allow me to exist, and so I do the same for him. I include him in the world.

I try to smile, and for the most part, I think I succeed.

We follow the accepted rules of conversational etiquette— one person talks, then another—and when it's my turn to talk, although they seem to be listening, what I'm saying doesn't seem to make much noise. And I don't really hear them either. I'm watching them, and I can see that they're moving their lips, but my response to whatever they're talking about, or the lack of it, doesn't seem to affect the conversation, or anyone's under-standing of the conversation. Somewhere along the line I see them whispering to each other. They turn to me and I get the idea that they've offered me a room for the night. I can feel my head nodding in affirmation, and my voice indicating that Yes, that would be nice. And more than the actual content of our speech, the meaning of the conversation is contained in the fact that by speaking to me they're acknowledging that at least I'm there.

3

So we all go home together, like a family, like Mom and Dad and Jack. They show me the house, and Geoff says, "Why don't you get your stuff." I tell him I don't have any stuff. And it's true. I'm wearing everything I own. Moving into the bedroom at the back of the house consists of walking in and sitting on the bed.

Geoff brings me into the master bedroom, their bedroom, and I can picture them lying in the big, newly made bed, loving each other, the laughter in the bed almost audible. To me. Not to Geoff, who opens some drawers in a dresser and brings out some pants and shirts and socks. He holds them out to me and I hold them against my body to check the fit. They're cleaner than my clothes and I begin wearing them. The pants have a stripe down the sides of the legs. The shirt is white, button-down. The shoes have a spongy insole.

Later, in a pair of borrowed pajamas, I sit on the edge of my bed, looking at the furniture: a dresser, a window, a lamp on a bedside table. The walls are white. A carved wooden bird hangs on a wall. I sit for a long time, forgetting that I'm sitting, and forgetting my breath, which is heavy and bumpy. My heart is beating as if catching up with something. There's an alarm clock beside the bed with bright green numbers that change into different numbers.

After a while I realize I've been sitting on the bed a long time. Like waking up, whatever I'd been doing on the bed before is gone, like an unremembered dream. If I was thinking, I don't remember what. And if I wasn't thinking, what was I doing? Whatever it was has faded away, and in waking, I come back to the world, worried that if I let myself go, I'll be gone entirely.

Days go by, or seem to, one day turning into another, and after a while—no one says anything—I seem to be living with them. Moving around the house, from kitchen to bedroom to bathroom, as we pass each other, I can feel my inconsequentiality. I'm not an obstacle to anything, but neither am I affecting the world in which they move. More and more I take long walks along the beach, or north of the beach, where the rocks start.

On certain nights Linda goes away to a class, and on one of those nights I find myself sitting on the sofa looking through an album of photographs, of Geoff and Linda on various vacations, and one of the photographs, with a lagoon in the background, freezes me. The two of them are standing in a jungle, looking at the camera, and you can actually see the happiness playing on their faces. I tell Geoff, who's reading a magazine, that it's a beautiful picture, thinking the expression of happiness, which lingers with me even when I look away, is something beautiful. I realize they've known each other for years, that their bond is strong. "Could I have a copy of this?" I ask him.

As I stare down at their faces full of happiness, full of transient joy, I see in the photograph, not only the happiness, but also the end of that happiness. As I continue staring at the fleeting moment revealed in the shiny piece of paper I can see the fleeting quality of everything, of life and the memory of life, and when I look up at Geoff, sitting in a chair in a room, it's like looking at a photograph. *Man with Crossed Legs*. The room and Geoff and even my act of looking are part of a fleeting moment which is over before it begins. I close the book of photos. "Never mind," I say. "But thanks."

A few days later, or hours later—I've lost track—I'm sitting on the same sofa. Geoff has gone to work so it must be during the day. Linda is stretching her legs on a mat near the wall in the living room. Light is coming in through the front windows and I sit, listening to her breathing, watching her on the blue mat in an exercise outfit, which, I imagine, wicks moisture away from her body.

I'm also looking at the rug on the floor and the shelves with boxes of music on the wall, and I'm pretty sure I'm sitting in a chair in a house in a city watching a person saluting an imaginary sun, moving her body into a variety of shapes. But because I'm not completely sure, and want some surety, I say something to Linda about something, it doesn't matter what because what I want is her attention. I want her to corroborate the world that seems to be the one I'm in. Because she's concentrating on something else, something other than the world we share, I stand up and walk to the closet. I find a vacuum cleaner and snap on a carpet attachment. I plug the cord into the wall and begin vacuuming the rug in the room where she's practicing.

I want to be in her thoughts, to exist in those thoughts, and so, although the rug is not that big, I keep vacuuming. She says something about not being able to concentrate, but I continue vacuuming. At which point she stands up and I think she has the intention of telling me to stop. But then she changes her mind. Some people are blessed with sympathy, and so she goes into the kitchen, finds a bucket of rags, grabs a handful, moistens them in the white sink and then hands me a rag and begins dusting. The windowsills and along the stereo shelves. I get on my hands and knees, and there's nothing like activity to distract the mind, and thank god for distraction I think as

I start scrubbing the floor and the baseboards, trying to get every last bit of dust and sand and hair. We're both doing it, working together, and the room is not boundless so we finish and move to the bedroom. There's a lot of dust there. I take the vacuum and she wipes down the woodwork. We make the bed, put away the dirty clothes, and we finish that room. Then the bathroom. The toilet needs scrubbing and the floor needs mopping and that's what we do. She polishes the mirror and the sink and I'm standing in the tub, using cleanser and sponge, cleaning the tiles and the area between the tiles, scrubbing off the mildew stuck to the porous grout. We work in a kind of unison, and it's hard to tell who's cleaning what, our various hands becoming a single pair of hands, scrubbing and rinsing and squeezing the sponge.

And then *she* steps into the tub. She kneels down and begins scrubbing the same tiles I've just polished, and I tell her, "I've already cleaned those tiles," but she keeps working, scraping away the discoloration. And that's when I realize that I haven't cleaned anything. I thought I was cleaning, and wanted to be cleaning, but I was just standing there the whole time, slightly off to the side, watching her. I thought I was holding a sponge, but when I look at my hand, nothing's there. I thought I was making some progress. I thought I was feeling connected to the world but instead of connected, I'm *dis*connected. And in the middle of that disconnection I seem hardly to exist.

I step out of the tub and follow Linda back to the kitchen. She puts the cleaning supplies under the sink. She goes to her rubber mat and begins where she left off with her yoga. She kneels down and then she stands on her head.

I watch her for a minute and I remember, from Alex, in Kentucky, one pose; it's the only pose I know but it's my favorite pose. I lie on my back, next to her, my legs stretched out and relaxed, my arms on the rug away from my hips, my eyes closed, my mind empty.

Not empty, but confined to my body, which is sinking into the floor. My eyes are relaxed. My mind is relaxed.

And then I stand up. Slowly. I roll over, then stand up, vertebra by vertebra, as much as I can. Once I'm up I notice that my senses seem to be functioning better. I can see with a little more acuity. I notice a dictionary on the stereo bookshelf. Two dictionaries, a paperback version next to a red hardcover. I pick up the frayed brown paperback, thumbing through, looking at the words and the black-and-white drawings beside the words. I ask Linda, standing on her head against the wall, if I can borrow the book.

She says nothing.

"I mean can I have it?"

I interpret her silence to mean I should take it.

I'm standing next to her, and I want to thank her, but because she's upside down, I'm standing next to her legs floating in the air. So I reach over—her ankles are showing—I reach over and I kiss her, lightly, on the skin of her ankle. And then I go to my room.

I sit on the bed.

My body is there. I can still feel my body, my butt bones on the mattress. I can feel my feet on the rug. I can feel the book in my hands, my fingers holding the weight of the book. I don't want to fade away. Fading away is frightening. I have things to do before I fade away.

So I stand up. I put on one of Geoff's dark blue sports coats, and in my borrowed clothes I leave the house. They live a few blocks from the water and I walk to the edge of the water, holding the dictionary against my wrist. When I watch the waves, although there are surfers riding the waves, all I can see is the water. The boardwalk, at that point along the coast, is just a sidewalk with cyclists and walkers and people on skates. I walk along with them, south toward the lifeguard tower, and keep walking, down past the coffee stand and along the sandy cement, the girls in bathing suits and boys in shorts. Surprisingly, I'm not in a hurry.

When I get to the Surfer Hotel I find the door to Polino's shack, the air-conditioning room where Polino and I used to sleep, and of course the door is locked. I find a thin piece of aluminum siding at the construction site next door and fit it between the door and the jamb and with a little jiggling I'm able to slip back the bolt on the door. I walk inside where it's cool, into the cinder-block hum of machinery. I go to the place behind the heater and find the box with the candle and the rolled-up blankets. I place the dictionary on the ground in front of the box, next to a valve with a tag hanging from the metal thread. I leave the book. No note, just the book.

4

I'm standing on a sidewalk at the side of a large supermarket. Cars are coming out of an underground parking garage. The world, as I notice it around me, has a clarity. Everything is clear, but also slightly removed. The outlines are sharp but the things themselves—the palm tree growing in the grass, the oil stains in the street, the sound of a motorcycle—all the things in the world are separate from me. Separate, and also the same. There's a certain pleasure in standing there, seeing the world in front of me, and not constantly wanting something from it all the time.

I would almost call it tranquillity, this lack of desire. Everything is just moving or not moving according to some plan, and because it's not my plan, and because I have no vested interest in the outcome, it seems perfect. And I want it to last. I want to keep feeling the perfection around me, and in me, but it can't go on forever, I think. Not like this.

So I stand there, and whatever it is, I feel it. I don't *try* to feel it, I just let it happen, and when I do, yes, the peace is there. The tranquillity is there, but I don't know. Is the peace of it all being over better than being in the world?

Wanting life *is* life, and I'm not quite ready to give it up. I don't want to be dead. I can adjust to anything, anything except not being. I still want to see what's going to happen. Maybe I'm greedy, but my habit is to hold on, so that's what I do.

And that's when the tranquillity starts to fade. I liked that tranquillity, but now it's replaced by the opposite of tranquillity, desire, a desire for the world. Without the world, and the tumult of the world, there's nothing. Not nothing*ness*. Just nothing. Without the world penetrating my senses, without that stimulation, there's only numbness. And although that numbness has a tranquillity component, it also has a black hole component. Which is why, as usual, I start walking.

I don't know what else to do. In an effort to keep from losing the world I wander along Mission Boulevard, along the narrow sidewalk, past the small pastel houses crowded together. I walk for what seems like a long time, until I come to the parking lot of the Mission Beach amusement park. I thought I was wandering aimlessly but maybe I had in my mind all along the idea of riding the roller coaster, because that's where I go.

Geoff had given me some spending money and so in the middle of the stalls and rides I find the ticket booth, buy a small red ticket, and wait in a line. As I'm standing there I notice a man who looks like my father, and who may well *be* my father, smoking a cigarette against a chain-link fence. Because my father is dead I watch this man as he takes a last puff, throws the butt on the ground, and walks away.

The line moves forward and a man in a sweatshirt tells a teenager in front of me to step into one of the cars. I step into an empty car behind him, and a metal bar is lowered over my chest. I'm sitting in the seat, and my car, part of a train of cars, starts moving. It's being pulled, slowly and deliberately, up the ramp, up to the highest point. I can hear the old metal wheels grating on the track. Then the silence of anticipation.

And then the car starts its plummet, and the rest of the ride is filled with the screams of excitement. But not my screams. During the ride, instead of excitement, I feel nostalgia. For life. This is life. You can't get much more adrenaline in life than this. And although the ride doesn't take much time, at the end of it I'm crying, not over the absence of that life, but over its existence.

5

It's the middle of the day and people are out, walking in the sun. I'm walking with them, watching them as they go about building their lives. I remember back to who I was with Anne, who I wanted to be with Anne, trying to build my life—and *our* life together—thinking I was building it, happy that I was there in the world, with her, although at the time I wasn't thinking about it, I was just doing it. It was my dream, and these people, I think, are also dreaming. Not *lost* in a dream, but dreaming of what can happen, dreaming of what life will mean, of who they want to be. Everyone wants to be something. I wanted to be something, but now I've forgotten what it was I wanted to be. I know it was something, something good, something that would make the world better, something that would make Anne happy.

Or maybe only *I* wanted to be happy? I'm not so sure. I'm not so sure my attraction to happiness included anyone other than me. I'm not convinced I wasn't alone the whole time Anne and I were together.

In New Jersey we were together. I know that. At the gas station. We'd been driving together, talking together, crossing the bridge together. Dreaming even. We had dreams: of children, of success, of friends, the garden, old age. Not too much about old age. We weren't there yet, but it was part of the dream, part of the implied dream we were dreaming together.

And now the dream is over. I didn't want it to be over before but now I remember what happened at the gas station. I was in the convenience store picking out candy bars and snack food, not just for me, but for her. I knew her, knew what she liked, and it was simple to choose those things that she liked. Which I did. I paid the woman at the counter and walked outside, into the cool air, into the daylight, and there she was, she'd thought of me, she'd pulled up near the door so I wouldn't have to walk so far. That was nice. I opened the door. I bent down and leaned in, put my hand on the seat. Look what I got, I started to say. I did say it, "Look what I got." And then I heard the sound, of the car. It wasn't making any noise but I knew it was there, moving. I heard it. I knew something was there and I was about to stand up. I saw what was about to happen.

And then it happened.

My head was in the car and my feet were on the pavement. A large car, a dark car, hit our car, and Anne died, and I also must have died.

I think that there ought to be more to the memory, but there isn't. I think there ought to be the recollection of every detail, every imperceptible detail of metal bending and bodies bending against the metal. Soft, pliable, broken bodies. There ought to be memories of lying on the ground, looking up at the sky growing darker and darker. There ought to be a life passing before my eyes, but it's not there.

It happened too quickly. And then it was over.

6

So this is it, I think. To be dead. To be dead and yet still holding on. In a way, I'm relieved. I've been fading away all this time, and now at least there's a reason.

As I walk up the street I look around, thinking that everything ought to be different, that the world would look and act and be a different thing. But the light poles are still light poles, and the dead grass is just what it is.

Coming home I find a note tacked to the door. It's a note with directions to a beach. I see the handwritten words on the paper and I'm surprised I can even make meaning from them. In a way they're just scribbles, just black lines and dots on a piece of paper. I fold the piece of paper, put it in my pocket, and then I go into the house.

I like the house, especially when it's empty. The windows are open. And it's clean. I remember trying to clean it. I remember everything, everything except the bird cage in the corner of the room. I step up to the metal cage and look inside. Where did this bird come from? Seeds and droppings are covering a newspaper at the bottom of the cage and I check to see if the bird has food. I touch the cage, and it's not an illusion. It's a canary. "Hi, Birdie," I say. I don't know the name of the bird so I call it Birdie. It's yellow and green, and when the bird starts singing I wonder, Why did I never notice this bird before? Like an imaginary world, which is now my world. And I don't mind. I sing along with the bird as best I can. If it *is* an imaginary world, at least, for a moment, it can be enjoyable.

I walk out of the house and down to the beach. I would say the walk to the beach is quiet, but it's not the sounds that are quiet. I feel light in my shoes. I find the spot where the note said they would be. And there they are, the two of them, together with other people, gathered around a fire. It's late afternoon. The sun is going down behind some clouds on the water.

I join the group and warm my hands at the fire. When I look at the fire, sometimes it seems to be a raging blaze and sometimes just the glowing of some embers. I don't know exactly which is the real fire, the embers or the blaze, but since I prefer the idea of a raging blaze that's what I see.

Linda is standing next to me. When she puts another log on I think, That's not a good idea. The fire is almost out of control as it is and it doesn't need another log. I try to tell her it doesn't need anything, but she doesn't hear me. She takes another log from the pile and sets it on what's already burning. I watch the embers crackle and spark, and I can see how the fire can change depending on how I look at it, that anything can change, depending on the attitude behind my eyes, and since now, in my mind, I'm making a roaring bonfire, I take a step back. I look at the rest of the people. They're wearing shorts and T-shirts, standing around the fire pit, focusing on the fire. Caught in the light of the fire they look animated, and although they don't know it, I am with these people, and it's nice to be with people.

Since they've brought marshmallows and coat hangers I find a coat hanger, straighten it out, and attach a marshmallow to the end of it. I dangle it over the fire. I may be dead, but I'm still going to roast a marshmallow. I hold it close to what I assume is the glowing heat. I'm bending over the fire pit when

Linda walks over to me. I watch her hand reach out and gently take the coat hanger from my hand. As if my hand wasn't even there. That's how I see it. The coat hanger slips easily into her fingers.

I say something to her.

It doesn't matter.

And that's when I say goodbye.

I feel the fading now, and rather than fight it, I'm ready to fade. I'm ready now to fade away completely.

When I say the word "Goodbye," more than actually saying it, I think it. To her. I think goodbye. I send some kind of feeling to her, and Linda senses that something is happening. She's holding the marshmallow skewer in one hand, and she looks in my direction. One last time. I look at her face, the face of a person living in the world. And then she bends over the fire.

They say that the readiness is all, and when I leave the circle and walk to a deserted part of the beach, I'm ready. I can hear the ocean, the waves of the ocean, the gentle waves. I can hear the voices of the people at the campfire being replaced by the sounds of the ocean. I face the sky, which is filled with color.

I like the sunset, and not just because it's the only time you can look directly at the sun. I like the light. I turn around and the side of the cliff is lit by the golden light. I see, near the base of the wooden stairs coming down the cliff, a shower, and someone washing sand off a boogie board.

They call it *painful* beauty because it's only here so long, and then it's over. Even when it's here, even as we experience it, it's over. And because I realize it's over, I'm holding on to that beauty, and even the sense of beauty, as long as I can.

I walk down to where the sand is wet and firm, away from the fires and the light. I take off my shoes and socks. I roll up my borrowed pants and take a step toward the water. A small wave trickles over my foot and my toes can feel the cold.

I would have thought that the temperature of the water wouldn't affect me, but it does. So I stay where I am, ankle-deep more or less, and just stand under the sky in the cold, moving water.

This must be what it is to be dead. Nothing much. It's just over. All of it. Even the beauty is over. I turn around, face the cliff.

I see Anne, standing at the base of the cliff. She's looking at me, holding her shoes in her hand. At first I don't believe it's her. But then she waves. I don't wave, but I walk out of the water and go to her. And when I get to her, there she is. White pants, yellow shirt. And it *is* Anne. I follow her up the wooden steps along the side of the cliff.

She begins walking along the grass at the lip of the cliff until she comes to a railing. She stops. She puts one hand on the railing. Her face is reflecting the light of the sun that's already set.

She's looking at me.

"You made it out," she says.

"I've been looking for you," I say.

"I'm here."

"It's warm here."

"It's summer," she says.

You wouldn't be able to hear her voice, but I can.

I take a deep breath.

"It's funny," I say, "seeing you here. It seems normal."

"Why not?" She smiles. "Look at the stars."

I look up at the sky, neither dark nor light. "It's too early to see any stars," I say.

"Some," she says, and she points to one, about halfway up. She was always good at finding stars.

She sits down on a cement bench overlooking the water. I wait while she puts her shoes on. I watch her tie the laces, and then we're walking again, side by side, not looking at each other. Occasionally a sentence or a word comes out of one of us.

"The air feels good," she says.

"I know," I say, and I feel the air, around me and in me, and—

7

You probably can't see us anymore, walking along the edge of the cliff. We're invisible now, although we don't quite know it.

We're walking. We know that. Our footsteps are very quiet. Our voices are silent.

And it's not a matter of accepting death. It doesn't happen like that. "Accepting" is a word in a dictionary and what happens isn't a word, just like clouds aren't words, or the man driving by with his arm out the window isn't a word.

But they happen. They all happen, and then they're gone.

Clouds, people, buildings, laughter, darkness. It all happens, and then it's gone. The piece of yellow paper in the street. The sounds of children in the distance. It fades away completely. The puddle in the sidewalk and the memory of the puddle.

And then it's gone.